Then it happened….

Lost in his grief, Dan almost missed the female hitchhiker by the side of the road. He slammed on the brakes; the car swerved and stopped next to her.

A tall, slim woman stood there. As he opened the door for her, a wonderful sense of euphoria seeped through him.

Kendra! Her face. Her smile. But most of all, eyes that held all of Kendra's secrets. He knew, he just *knew*. She smiled at him as if she understood exactly what he was feeling and thinking.

He was going crazy. He had just visited Kendra's grave.

All of their hopes and dreams had died with his wife.

Until now….

Dear Reader,

When I was very young, I didn't understand what the word *love* really meant. Instead I used it freely to describe whatever struck my fancy as a teenager—including TV shows and fast foods! Whenever one of my friends fell in love with a boy, though, I thought it was just plain dumb. Until it happened to me.

I'll never forget the intensity of that moment. I was seventeen and had a date with an older boy. We went to his fraternity party and danced through the evening. Later, when we kissed, I actually heard those bells and whistles that people write about! I thought I'd died and gone to heaven. Our love carried us through and we married and had four wonderful children.

But sometimes the dream doesn't always work out. With all the pressures of life, of raising four children, somehow those same two people who had grown together also grew apart. We divorced.

I became depressed. I felt I was too old for love, that the dream of one true love was childish. But I must have liked something about romance, because I wrote about it and dreamed about it! And then my other single friends, one by one, proved me wrong by finding Mr. Right for *them*.

I realized I was wrong—that romance has to be part of us our whole lives in order for our souls to breathe. That idea lead to this, my most fantastical story, where Dan and Kendra, two extremely unlikely lovers, learn the unexpectedness and power of love.

And now I know that there is no answer in life unless it's a simple four letter word.

Love.

Rita Clay Estrada

FORMS OF LOVE

BY

RITA CLAY ESTRADA

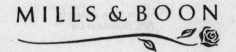

MILLS & BOON

All the characters in this book have no existence outside the imagination of the author, and have no relation whatsoever to anyone bearing the same name or names. They are not even distantly inspired by any individual known or unknown to the author, and all the incidents are pure invention.

MILLS & BOON and the Rose Device are trademarks of the publisher.
TEMPTATION is a trademark of Harlequin Enterprises Limited, used under licence.
This edition published by arrangement with Harlequin Enterprises B.V.
First published in Great Britain in 1995
by Harlequin Mills & Boon Limited, Eton House, 18-24 Paradise Road,
Richmond, Surrey TW9 1SR

© Rita Clay Estrada 1994

ISBN 0 263 79369 9

21 - 9507

Printed in Great Britain by
BPC Paperbacks Ltd

Prologue

KENDRA LOVEJOY stood in the lobby of the theater, hardly noticing the jostling crowd about her. She'd found the answer she'd been looking for. How strange to find the solution in an old movie.

It was time for her to take control of her life again. To risk. For the past two years she'd been a coward, pretending everything was going to get better without her making any of the needed changes.

She exited the theater and was surrounded by a group of strangers. Everyone paused at the curb, waiting for the light to change so they could cross to the parking lot on the other side of the street. Kendra's car was there, too, but she wasn't ready to return to her parents' home just yet. Her mind was full of images and feelings that needed to be clarified. She needed to put them in some kind of order—as her therapist had suggested.

An older woman beside her patted her male companion's arm sympathetically. "I know, honey. The first time I saw *An Affair to Remember*, I felt overwhelmed, too," she said. Kendra looked at the man, wondering what the woman saw there. To her, the man looked bored.

Kendra didn't move until someone bumped into her on their way across the street. She stepped back, leaning against the building as she tried to calm the powerful tide of feelings that was washing over her.

Glancing up and down the San Antonio street glowing gold with late-afternoon sunshine, she spotted a doughnut shop a few doors away. She'd go there and take some time to sit and work her ideas through. The movie had brought so many emotions to the surface, adding to her already-confused state. She needed to be alone and to make some decisions.

Two minutes later she was esconced in a window booth with fresh coffee and an éclair in front of her. Relishing each bite of the pastry, she considered her life.

After two years of separation from Dan and after months of counseling twice a week, it was time to make a decision that only she could make. Could she go back to Dan and begin a new life—on her terms?

One emotion stood out—and it had everything to do with all the other emotions that swamped her. That emotion was love—love for Dan.

She had loved him since the first time she'd seen him, when they were in junior high school. She'd been his best friend ever since; and his love and his lover until she'd walked away from it all two years ago.

Dan had never been able to give her the kind of love she needed. He had such a strong personality that he had simply taken over.

At the time, Kendra had felt that she had no choice but to follow him. He became the focal point of her entire existence. After several years, she'd found herself practically unable to function independently. After the death of their infant daughter, however, she had to leave Dan. She'd felt it was the only way she could survive.

She'd told him she had to "find herself," even though she had no idea what the expression meant at the time. All she cared about was getting away from him before she suffocated.

Now, two years later, she knew what that overused expression meant.

Finding herself meant she had to learn to form her own opinions and to stand up for them. To discover her taste in clothing, music, books—in a life-style. To make her own decisions about what she wanted and valued most in life.

Finding out who she was also meant dealing with the overwhelming emotions that claimed her from time to time; learning how to cope with the dark thoughts and depression that assailed her. Easier said than done, she thought, taking another bite of her éclair. But she was finally learning how to do it. Like now.

It felt good. She felt powerful.

In a week Dan would return to Houston from Israel and come to San Antonio to see her. Ever since their separation, he'd accepted three-month engineering contracts, working in the Middle East, Africa and Europe. And after the end of each job he'd return to San Antonio and ask Kendra to come back to him. After her tearful refusal, he would leave, setting out for Big Bend country, where he rafted down the river as if it would wash all his heavy burdens away. In a sense she was sure that it did.

During Dan's visits, they always argued. He would demand to know *when* she would be ready, and she would always say she didn't know.

This time, though, her answer would be different.

This time, she wanted to be part of his life, and not just part of him.

She also wanted to get pregnant and have another baby, despite the fact that she would be afraid of losing a second child to SIDS. Her darling baby girl had been four months old when sudden infant death syndrome had taken her from them. Kendra stopped those thoughts. Painful as it had been, she could do nothing to change that event. Only the future could be affected. She had some control there, and the place to start was with Dan.

She wanted both to be able to stand with Dan, and to stand up to him, too.

She wanted to make love to him when *she* felt like making love, not just when he reached for her.

She wanted some control in their relationship, and she knew now that she had to reach out and grasp it, not wait until Dan handed it to her. She, and she alone, was responsible for her decisions—or lack of them.

Though exhilarated, she was also frightened by the power she felt flowing through her. It was a new and wondrous feeling.

She wanted...

Kendra put down her coffee cup and stared out the window at the slowly darkening streets. She wanted so much, and it was only now that she was finally willing to fight for it.

And the stakes were so simple. If she succeeded in taming Dan, she had everything to win: love, family, a full life. If she failed, she was no worse off than she was now: alone, lonely and scared of everything including her own shadow. She had everything to gain and nothing to lose.

A small smile tugged at her mouth. It had taken two years to come to such a simple decision.

What was wrong with wanting a love that was as strong as the one in *An Affair to Remember*? And she wanted it with Dan.

He loved her with all his heart—she knew that. And he wanted her back in his life—she knew that. He would always be overbearing, but the few times she'd stood up to him, he'd listened and weighed her opinion as if it mattered. He hadn't always agreed, but then who did?

A heady feeling washed over her. Yes!

She had all the ingredients for a deep and abiding relationship that would endure the test of time.

So, what was she doing here?

The need for immediate action gripped her like a vise. Unable to sit still for one more second, Kendra stood, placed a tip on the table and walked through the swinging glass door. The sun had almost disappeared behind the buildings on the far side of the street.

With steps that were sure and a feeling of excited anticipation flowing through her veins, she almost jogged to the corner. It was the middle of the night in Israel, and Dan would be sleeping. Good. She wanted to call right away. He needed to know now that she was willing; that she wanted to be with him for the rest of her life—but that there were terms he needed to be apprised of. *Her* terms. She had no doubt that he'd balk, but he'd come around eventually. He had to, for both their sakes.

Impatiently, she waited for the light to change. The people who had been milling about earlier were gone, another showing of the movie had begun.

Kendra stepped off the curb and into the street. By the time she saw the flash of gray, it was too late.

She was pitched into the air, her body hit the front windshield, then rolled until she slammed onto the pavement. At first she was stunned. Then she realized she was numb. She tried to move, to stand, but her limbs refused to obey her command. Car doors slammed, people shouted.

"It wasn't my fault!" a deep, west Texas accent insisted. "She just walked out in the middle of the street. Right in front of me! I slammed on my brakes, but it was too late!"

Kendra felt like two people. One part of her was detached from the pain she was sure was there. The observer listened to the others and tried to interpret their sounds and tones. The other part of herself tried to tell them she had to call Dan, but she couldn't even open her eyes. A low moan came from somewhere inside her and she realized that she was slipping away from the voices. *No! She didn't want to die!* Not when she had a chance of putting her life together!

A soothing force entered her mind and subdued her agitated thoughts.

I have to tell Dan, Kendra began again.

If you allow us, we'll help you through this, the presence explained.

Help me get up and leave here!

We can't do that. You're dying.

No! Not now! Not when I'm so close to . . . Tears slipped from between her closed eyelids and down her cheeks.

Tell us what you want him to know, the voice pursued. *We promise he will know.*

Memories of their life together, so intertwined with her deepest emotions, flashed through Kendra's mind. The last six months of her life and the realization that she had been loved by the man she loved were enough. *I love him so much,* she thought hazily, realizing she was losing touch with the voices around her. The wail of an ambulance came closer, but she focused all her waning attention on the force that was hearing her thoughts. *I wish you could take my thoughts to him as a gift. It wasn't that he was so strong. It was that I was so weak.*

We can. We will, was the reply. The soothing force seemed to stroke her as if she were a baby, and she finally relaxed. She couldn't do more. Kendra had the utmost faith that whoever it was would give Dan her messages.

Everything else slowly faded away. Instead of feeling the hard, hot pavement beneath her, Kendra seemed to rise. She watched in awe and fascination as everyone scurried back and forth over a body that looked just like her.

Inquisitive, she glanced around the rest of the area, spotting what looked like an abandoned used-car lot. She was sure the person who had comforted her stood near the doorway of the trailer office. In this unusual, suspended state she understood so much; the person was one body with a collective mind. How unusual. Even as she watched, the body was changed into a female similar to Kendra in appearance. That would make it easier for "her" to find Dan and explain things to him. To ease his way. To love him.

Kendra smiled.

Wait. Don't go yet, the soother said.

It's too late, Kendra replied. *You know what to say. You promised*.

WHEN THE ACCIDENT occurred on the side street just off Broadway in downtown San Antonio, Texas, we knew this was the form we, I, would assume.

After her death, we would blend into the population and no one would know we were here.

In the dwindling light we curled our pudgier body into a ball just out of sight of the small group of gawking motorists, finding sanctuary in the deep-set office doorway of a used-car lot. Our highly tuned, telepathic waves scanned the frantic inner cries of the wounded woman sprawled on pavement still warm from the late-afternoon sun. Our own thoughts wrapped around her chaotic thoughts. While soothing her frantic cries we absorbed her memories, making them our own. With the careful precision taught over a lifetime, we altered our own state and began weaving our image into the slightly different and very pretty form that was hers.

Finished with the physical attributes, we began absorbing the mental processes. We were now growing tired and the woman lying in the middle of the road was rapidly weakening. We tried to hold on to her thoughts, to help calm her so that we could absorb them properly, but her will to live was slipping, slipping. . . .

Suddenly she was dead, and we hadn't fully completed the transformation. Unemotionally, we thought of the alternatives. Should we seek another specimen? We searched our new memory banks. We had all her memories of the last six months. That should be enough to get us through the next two weeks—the maximum time allotted for the mission.

Slowly, we stood on our new legs. We tested their strength by bouncing up and down on the balls of our much larger feet. We felt strange but good.

Flexing our hands, we watched the smooth skin over our slim fingers and knuckles tighten and loosen. The fingers were long and supple. This body was obviously a good choice.

Reaching down inside a small bag we had been carrying for the past three days we pulled out an oversize, bulky-knit sweater, a pair of drawstring pants and a pair of thongs—all chosen with the purpose of fitting almost any body style. Also inside the lining were forged papers that would help us identify ourselves to other humans—just in case it was necessary.

When dressed, we looped the bag on our shoulder and looked down the road toward the city lights, where a strip of restaurants and bars littered the sides of the street. Our mouth moved, softly uttering our new name into the darkness.

Kendra Lovejoy.

As the ambulance activated its siren and headed toward the nearest hospital with its lifeless cargo, the we that was now Kendra Lovejoy stepped out of the shadows and headed toward the lights of the nearest bar. We hummed a popular song that spoke of lost love, cheap whiskey and girls who do men wrong.

It was time to begin.

1

WHEN DAN LOVEJOY awoke, he glanced around the room, reacquainting himself with the apartment he'd called home base since Kendra had left him. Most of the time he was out of the country, so he'd never bothered doing much to make the place a home.

The bedroom was sparsely furnished, with a bed, a dresser and an old chair. There were no paintings on the walls, no knickknacks, no personal touches except for the few clothes in the closet and items that spilled from his suitcase on the floor. The living room was no different. And piled in one corner sat three boxes of books, awards and citations, never unpacked.

Suddenly he craved more.

He'd been offered a permanent job overseas, and for the first time since Kendra had left him he was considering it. By now he should have stopped hoping that Kendra would return to him. Every night he dreamed of her miraculous cure and of their being together again. And every morning he faced the disappointment of waking up alone.

He rolled to the side of the bed and sat up. The small slip of white paper sent to him from the Israeli office headquarters last week was now tucked securely in his jacket pocket. He hadn't received the damn thing until just before flight time.

The message that he should call had come from Kendra's parents in San Antonio—a disturbing element in itself, since they rarely contacted him unless they had bad news or needed money.

Just then the phone rang and he jumped, glancing at his watch. He'd slept without waking for twenty-one hours. Nerves that had finally relaxed in sleep were once more tense and ready for action. He answered it on the fifth ring.

"Dan! I'm so glad you're back!" Ed, Kendra's father, sounded relieved.

A new growth of beard made Dan's jawline itch, and he rubbed his callused hand over it. "Thanks. I was going to call you in just a couple of minutes. My flight routing was screwed up and it took two days to get home. I didn't get in until late. What's up?" He tried to sound casual.

"It's Kendra." Ed's voice broke into a sob. Dan's hand tightened around the receiver. "She's dead, Dan. My little Kendra is gone. Damn! I still don't believe it!"

Dan heard the words but they made no sense. He couldn't have heard right. It couldn't be. No! Ed didn't know what he was saying. His mind's eye formed a picture of his beautiful wife—just as alive and vibrant as sunshine. The woman he loved with all his heart. Nothing could happen to her. He wouldn't allow it.

"What are you talking about, Ed?" he finally managed.

The older man's voice cracked two or three times before he finally pushed the story out. "Kendra went to a twilight movie and when she came out, she...she got hit by a car. She just stepped off the curb, Dan. Witnesses said she didn't look left or right. She...she just stepped into this car's path and died five minutes later." The older man began crying again.

Dan stared at the bare wall, seeing instead a beautiful, laughing Kendra. "When?"

"Six days ago. She'd just got word that you'd be back soon and we were all so happy. The psychiatrist was sure Kendra had finally made a major breakthrough. She was looking forward to seeing you again. She even talked of trying to make amends, to see if there was a chance your marriage could work." He took a shaky breath. "She was so hopeful. We were positive this was the end of the nightmare...."

Dan's stomach felt like a giant fist was squeezing it. He swallowed, then swallowed again to ease the tightness. It didn't help. Kendra. His Kendra. Gone. It couldn't be. It couldn't be!

"Ed," he began, but his thoughts refused to turn into words that would convey his emotions.

"I know," the older man choked. "There's nothing you can say. It's done. I'm sorry, Dan. We worked so hard for so long to make everything right, but God wouldn't let us. We were almost there—" His voice broke completely. "My baby. My only baby."

Dan's throat closed. He swallowed, this time tasting bile that was rising to close off his windpipe. "I'll call you later." He slammed the phone back on the hook and ran for the kitchen to throw up in the sink. He wished he could just as easily purge the despair, the unbelievable ache that spread through his body.

His hand clenched against his heaving stomach. It hurt. Damn! It hurt so damn bad he wanted to break his ribs, pull out his heart and throw it away.

Then the tears began in unstoppable torrents. And with the tears came sobs that tore his soul apart. In the dimly lit apartment, he sat on the kitchen floor and held his buzzing head. In the past two years all he'd asked for was one more chance to give Kendra whatever it was she needed to want to stay with him. After all, they'd lost so much when they'd lost their baby. How much misery and pain could two people survive? Just one more chance. In a crazy world filled with chaos, he hadn't thought it too much to ask. He'd been wrong.

"STEADY, BOY, YOU'RE doing fine." Kendra soothed the young airman leaning against her in the curved booth of the dimly lit bar.

"You're so b'u'iful," he muttered against the soft skin of her breast above the scooped neckline of a cotton T-shirt. She chuckled because she was supposed to.

"So are you," she said dryly. "Beautiful and drunk."

"I love you." Once more his lips tried to caress the soft flesh above her breast. Instead, his sloppy mouth smeared her with spittle and she shuddered.

"I don't think either one of us knows what that emotion is really like, bucko."

"It's how I feel, you," the drunk hiccuped, sliding his hand up her thigh until her hand held his in place.

She edged away, letting his head drop to the booth seat. "Sorry, Larry, but my time is up. It's time to go home now."

He tried to sit up but failed miserably and leaned on one arm instead. "Home?" His bleary eyes tried to focus on her face. "Where's home?"

Reaching for her large canvas purse where her specimens were, she smiled and slid out of the booth. "Mine's a lot farther away than yours."

"Don't go," he said in a last-ditch attempt to keep her with him.

"I have to, and thank you for your kind donation." There was that odd sense of humor again. It slipped out occasionally. She wasn't sure if it was hers, or the original Kendra's.

She left the bar and stepped out into the darkened parking lot. Taking a deep breath, she stared at the heavens, wishing the answers she sought would be written up there. There were too many city lights to see the stars clearly, and she had to guess the exact direction of her planet.

Something else was different with her. Kendra had met one of her kind yesterday, who was failing her own mission. Instead of feeling compassion, Kendra had felt smug. Her fellow team member hadn't found an opportunity to collect a single DNA sample. Whereas Kendra had found four strong, handsome males and had gotten samples from all of them.

Tonight she had shuddered when the airman's spittle touched her skin. That was an emotion, a human response. Was she adapting to the human condition more quickly than she should? Perhaps her body was too tired to help her right now. She would spend one more night in the hotel room she'd rented, then hitchhike back to the vastness of west Texas—and the mother ship cradled inside a mountain—tomorrow afternoon.

Having promised the dead Kendra that she would tell her man how she felt about him—that elusive emotion called love—the new Kendra set out to find him. She located the woman's parents—and had *malked* them—mind-talking, earthlings would call it. According to Ed's understanding, Dan should be in San Antonio by now. If she didn't contact him by tomorrow, she'd be forced to leave without fulfilling her promise.

Surprisingly, the promise was becoming more and more important to her the longer she spent on Earth. One way or another, she'd find Dan Lovejoy.

He'd be in for quite a shock, that odd sense of humor suggested once again.

AS THE MORNING SUN came over the tall pines of northwest Houston, Dan finished loading his black Jeep four-wheel drive with deliberate efficiency. No matter how busy he tried to keep himself, however, memories of Kendra intruded. More so as he jumped in the Jeep and headed west toward San Antonio.

Toward Kendra's grave.

Thoughts of her carried him over the miles, eating time so easily they made the long trip seem like the passage of a few minutes.

Kendra. Kendra. Kendra.

His mind returned to the first time he saw her....

Her hair seemed black as night until she moved into the sun; then it glinted like coal shot through with veins of copper. She stood at the edge of a crowd in the junior high schoolyard, where he was trying to punch out a guy who'd teased him about his weight. He looked up and saw her. Her head was tilted inquisitively to the side as she silently watched the adolescent display. His opponent took advantage of Dan's distraction, flattening him with a solid fist to the stomach.

Because of that first glimpse of Kendra's dark-haired beauty, Dan had gone on a diet the very same day, never to be heavy again.

Kendra . . . When he took her to the junior-senior prom, he could hardly keep his hands off her. In his eyes, she was the loveliest girl there. Draped in a long gown of off-white and pale peach, she looked like an angel. That night, before taking her home, he parked the car on a remote road. She was patient with his fumbling beneath her dress. For the first time since they'd been dating, he tasted the sweetness of her breast and thought he'd gone to heaven.

Kendra . . . after their high school graduation when he drove her to a motel room and impatiently made love to her for the very first time. She had quietly cried—and so had he. But he had felt like a man at last.

Kendra . . . visiting his senior college apartment in Austin and tearfully telling him of her pregnancy. They ran to a justice of the peace, then, and a month later had a formal wedding. It was filled with parents' friends as both sides of the family celebrated the "youngsters" finally getting together. Two weeks later, Kendra lost the baby. It took several years for her to become pregnant again.

Kendra . . . three years ago, as she sat in the new rocker and stared out the nursery window for hours at a time after losing four-month-old Hannah. The first night, they had cried together. Hannah had been the most beautiful black-haired, blue-eyed baby. They loved and missed her so much. . . .

San Antonio loomed on the horizon and Dan forced himself to cut off the memories. A quick stop-off at Ed and Margaret's, a visit to Kendra's grave, then he'd head for west Texas and try to find some peace.

He turned onto Loop 410 south. Without realizing it, he lifted his foot off the gas. Kendra lived just minutes from here. No, not Kendra. Kendra's parents.

He forced himself to push down on the pedal. He had to get this over with.

He had to . . .

IT WAS NOON BEFORE Kendra checked out of her motel room and walked down the sidewalk, her bag swinging from her shoulder. Her step was jaunty. Her eyes took in the vivid and colorful wonders of the human world. In two or three days she'd be on the mother ship and on her way home. All this fabulous, if too exciting, color-brightness would be gone.

A feeling resembling regret flowed through her, but she reined it in. This was not her planet—not the world for her. Peace was at home, not here, where barbaric customs practiced by a barbaric race abounded.

The highway to Del Rio was six miles away, but she decided to walk because she loved this newfound strength in her legs and torso. It felt so *free* to stride on legs that were long and strong! At home, we—she stopped and substituted the human language equivalent—she would glide slowly and be more tied to the ground's much stronger gravity.

Once more she tried to reach a communicator or Guardian with whom she could share information. She concentrated on sending out her message and once again, there was no answer. It was odd, but she wasn't going to worry, yet; it could be the fault of not having absorbed all of Kendra's memories. She sighed into the dark night air. Her people didn't know as much about Earth as they thought they did.

When she'd landed, she believed that her teachers and the training tapes had supplied all the information she would need. That hadn't been the case. Once here, she'd been working with a combination of her own common sense and Kendra's knowledge, because the methods she was taught at home weren't always practical in the "field."

DAN STOOD AT Kendra's grave, still hardly believing it was really hers. The grass had been dug up as if a giant bird had scarred the earth with its talons, exposing the rich, damp darkness of newly turned loam.

Next to Kendra's marker was a marble statue of an angel with outspread wings guarding a lush, green carpet of freshly cut grass. Encased in glass at the base of the monument was a picture of Hannah just one day before her fourth month birthday. She looked smiling and happy and ready to return all the love her parents could give her. It was a heartbreakingly beautiful picture, and the main reason that Dan didn't come to the grave site too often.

It hurt so damn much to lose someone you love once.

It was killing him to lose someone he loved *twice*.

As hard as he tried to stop them, the tears streamed down his face. Sobs tore at his throat as he told the two females he loved just how much he missed them. How dare they leave him here to fend for himself, alone?

If only he'd had one more chance to prove how much he loved them. Just one . . .

Dan left Kendra's grave with reluctant steps. At last he accepted that Kendra was really dead and this was not some cruel, bizarre joke.

This was no dream. This was a waking, breathing, living nightmare.

With his mind on automatic pilot, he headed toward Highway 90 and the small border town of Del Rio. His hands clenched the steering wheel tightly until aching biceps reminded him to ease his grip. His brain seemed to be wrapped in cotton, buffering the shock of the past two days. Knowing that the pain would soon return, he gratefully accepted and embraced the momentary numbing of his emotions.

Glancing at the gas gauge, he focused on the mundane. Gas and an oil check were in order since he only had a quarter of a tank left. It might as well get done now, so he wouldn't have to stop once he hit the main stretch of highway. He pulled into the right-hand lane and watched for the nearest exit.

Then it happened. His mind froze for just a moment; next he felt as if someone had nudged him. He saw an image of Kendra's lifeless body lying in the road. He blinked once. Then twice. His foot slammed on the brake, almost pulling the squealing Jeep into the flow of heavy traffic again.

Blinking again, he noticed a tall, slim woman stood by the side of the road. Her long dark hair was the color of coal with jets of copper glinting in the late-afternoon sun. The smile tilting her mouth upward was as familiar to him as his own face in the mirror. The neatly printed cardboard sign in her hand proclaimed she was heading toward Big Bend country in west Texas. For just a fleeting moment, he saw the words *Hi, Dan* written there. Impossible!

And he couldn't refuse to pick her up. A small back section of his mind screamed at him to pass her by, leave her alone. But he stopped the Jeep anyway.

A wonderful, novocaine-type euphoria seeped through every pore. He was soaked with wonderful, soothing feelings and he couldn't resist falling under their spell. He wanted to cry with the poignant sweetness of it.

He flipped the door lock and pushed the door open. "Get in."

Kendra! Her face. Her smile. But most of all, eyes that held all of Kendra's secrets. He knew, he just *knew*. She was two feet away from his truck, her head tilted in that disarmingly funny way. She smiled at him as if she knew exactly what he was feeling and thinking.

He was going insane.

His heart was thumping so fast, he hurt from the effort of breathing. His breath was ragged. His ears buzzed.

She stood very still. "Are you sure you're prepared for this?"

"Get in," he repeated. It was all he could say.

He watched her grasp the side of the door and swing into the passenger seat. Every movement, every nuance was Kendra's. Not so much in appearance, although they were similar, but in essence. He didn't know how he knew, he just knew.

It *was* Kendra!

She sighed, leaning back against the upholstery. "It's hotter than Hades out there right now." Her eyes closed for a moment, then opened and looked back at him. Deep, liquid, familiar brown eyes that were calm and reassuring. "You're Dan."

He nodded, unable to piece together a single sentence. The novocaine was wearing off and he was filling with chaotic thoughts. Tears glazed his eyes. This had to be a dream, a figment of his imagination.

"Who are you?" he finally managed.

"Kendra."

"Kendra's dead. Who are you?"

"Oh, dear." She sighed. "I forgot I've got to explain all this before we can get on with the business at hand."

"Who are you?" he repeated.

"Drive." She waved toward the highway. "We can talk while you get us where we're going." She tilted her head again, her big brown eyes regarding him steadily. "Isn't it lucky that you're on your way to Big Bend, too? I don't have to waste extra time tracking you down."

He nodded again, automatically putting the Jeep in gear. Something told him to wait and he'd get the answers he demanded. Every two seconds he looked in her direction, fully expecting her to have disappeared.

"Who are you?" he repeated. His voice was a belligerent croak. He didn't care.

"Would you believe I'm Kendra's twin?"

"No."

"What would you believe?"

"That I miss Kendra so much, I'm hallucinating." What the hell was he doing arguing with his own imagination? This couldn't really be happening. It couldn't! Ed and Margaret had identified Kendra's body. But he so badly wanted to see Kendra again, to explain his feelings, to hear her tell him how and why their once intimate and cozy world had fallen apart, that . . .

She turned in the seat, crooking one leg up and placing an arm over the back of the seat. "Let's just say that I'm a figment of your imagination, Dan. I can listen to your thoughts and give you the answers you need. When we reach Big Bend, I'll disappear. Then you'll resume your life, but I'll erase all memory of me from your mind. You'll remember Kendra, but not me."

Her voice was barely a whisper but he had no trouble hearing her. He let his breath out in relief. He wasn't crazy; he just needed to control his screwed-up emotions, pick up the pieces of his life and go on. This must be his way of coping. Unless . . .

"Kendra's dead, Dan. She died just as Ed and Margaret said she did. She was hit by a car outside a movie theater."

"How? Why?" His eyes flickered to her, then back to the road again.

"Because she wasn't looking where she was going. She was thinking of other things. All of them had to do with you."

"How do you know?" His hand hit the steering wheel. "Shit! I'm crazy as a loon! You're not even here! This is all some goddamn reaction to jet lag."

"Don't you want the answers? I can give them to you, you know. Kendra asked me to."

She was still here—even after his denial of her. And her eyes were probing his mind. Those eyes . . .

He was compelled to ask. "What was she thinking about me?"

"She thought that you were a better person than she was. She wanted to make it up to you for all the grief she'd caused in the past two years. And she hoped you two would have a chance to start again."

Dan shook his head. "What the hell's going on here? I don't understand." Frustration and anger lined his face. "Dammit! I don't understand!"

She shrugged, facing forward. "Take it easy. After all, this is all new to me, too, Dan. Training didn't cover half the situations I've had to cope with this past week. But if you don't want to know—"

"Know what?"

"The answers to those questions you've asked yourself over and over. Every time you're alone with nothing to do, you quiz yourself on where you went wrong. You've come up with a thousand different answers, but it never dawned on you to look at *both* halves of the whole. You just accepted that Kendra couldn't be the one at fault."

"She wasn't," he said automatically.

"Shame on you," she chided. "You're old enough to know that no one is ever all right or all wrong. Least of all, Kendra. Don't forget she was the only child of doting parents. She'd never had to deal with much adversity, so she hadn't learned how to be strong. Before Hannah's death, she led you around by the nose most of the time."

"That's not true."

"I don't know why, but you always thought you must have done something wrong that you weren't ever aware of. You always thought you'd done something so hideous that it drove her away."

The depth of her perception hit him hard.

"Get some gas, Dan, before we run out."

He snapped his attention back to her. Had he heard the words aloud or only in his mind? She sat calmly next to him, her eyes on the road, her expression a pleasant blank.

With a silent obedience foreign to him, he pulled off the highway and into a self-serve gas station. After a long look at his passenger, he stepped out of the Jeep and began the process of filling the tank and checking the oil. All the while he kept an eye on his rider, wondering when she would disappear and he would come to his senses.

Climbing into the driver's seat, he stared at her. She was still there, waiting calmly for him to continue the trip. Twisting the key in the ignition, he ground the starter until it caught, then shifted the vehicle into gear and pulled into traffic. He kept his passenger within his peripheral vision. His mind started to work again.

He remembered something she'd said earlier. "What training?"

"We have tapes that teach us your human customs. They give us everyday knowledge of earthly expressions, history and current events."

His gaze darted to hers. "What are you?"

Kendra leaned back and smiled at the brightness of the sun hitting the dash. "I'm a Herfronite."

"What the hell is that?" Frustration swamped him again. Everything was out of control—including his mind.

"Herfron is a planet one galaxy away."

Slamming on the brakes, he brought the Jeep to a halt on the shoulder of the road. He turned and reached for the slim shoulders next to him. But when he touched her, his hands immediately gentled to a caress.

"Don't hurt me, Dan. Never hurt me."

His fingers sought and found her birdlike collarbones. "What would you do if I beat you?"

Her large brown eyes stared up at him so calmly he could have got lost in them. "Put you to sleep instantly, then I would leave and let you awaken with no memory of anything that happened to you over this past week. You'd have to learn of Kendra's death all over again and go through the pain of seeing her parents, her grave."

"You could do that?" He stared into her eyes, mesmerized by their soporific effect on him.

"Yes. Although I've never done it before, the training tapes taught us the methods to use."

He believed her. "How?"

"I can tranquillize your mind, then erase what I want or substitute some other actions." She shrugged and he felt her muscles tighten and respond. "I knew you were coming and pulled you over to pick me up. Didn't you feel that compulsion?"

"I saw Kendra." He searched her face again. "But you're not her. You resemble her, but you're not her."

"Right. But her memories of the past six months are mine. I was there when she died and I absorbed her memories and emotions. I tried to soothe those last moments for her." She smiled sweetly, proud of her accomplishments. "I think I did."

"Why did you find me?"

"Because she asked me to tell you about her thoughts and wants. I promised I would do so."

"Why would you do that? Why not just promise and then cut and run?"

"We keep our promises." She furrowed her brow. "We aren't supposed to promise anything to anyone down here, but she was so . . . so adamant."

"This is ridiculous," he stated once more. It was easier to deny this conversation than to accept it.

A new thought entered his head and wouldn't let go. "Did you kill her?" His hands tightened on her shoulders. He didn't know how he knew, he just knew she would allow him to force her only so far.

"No. I was just in the right place at the right time." Her hands covered his. "She was my connection to a human personality."

Connection? Nothing in this conversation made sense.

"She was the human I needed to create a human identity while here on Earth," she explained.

"But you're not human, dammit!" His fingers tightened again.

"No, We are Mais—a third-generation mixture. Our planet is the leader in math and engineering. Our species is mentally brilliant but physically weak. We began looking for a race we could mix with, a race that would contribute their strength while we retain our own intelligence, our mental powers. We've been working on it for the past hundred years and with the help of good DNA engineering, we're finally succeeding."

"You mean—" Dan's mind whirled as he stared at her features, the texture of her skin, the freckles on her nose. . . .

"I mean that genetically I'm a human, mentally I'm a Herfronite." She shrugged lightly and his hands dropped from her shoulders. He didn't know whose will dictated it, but they now lay in his lap.

"I'm crazy. I'm really crazy."

"No," she soothed, stroking his arm. "But you're exhausted. Why don't you let me drive for a while and you sleep in the back seat?"

"No! I'll drive."

"As you wish." She faced forward again, waiting for him to begin driving. No games, no pretending. She just took him at his word.

He put the car in gear and once more edged onto the paved road. A sign said Castroville 30 Mi. If he wasn't crazy and this woman beside him really was what she claimed, he could pull into that town and ask for help. He almost grinned at the thought of running into a police station and yelling about invaders from outer space. It sounded like something out of a bad science fiction movie. They'd think he was nuts!

He drove in silence for half an hour before hitting the outskirts of Castroville. Should he pull in?

It would do no good except to discredit you, Dan, a voice in his head said. It was clear as a bell, each word crisp with meaning; it was *her* voice.

He looked at her. "You did that," he accused.

She nodded.

"How?"

"It's called *malking.* I speak to your mind."

"Can I do it?"

"To me? Yes. To others of your race? Not yet, although you're only about five hundred years away from doing so."

"How do you know?"

She lifted her brows, obviously surprised he could ask such a question. "Our training tapes said so."

"Ah, yes. The training tapes. You mentioned that you were part human. Third generation. Then why do you call yourself a Her—?"

"Herfronite?"

"Yes. Explain it to me."

"Your scientists have been seriously playing with genetics for the past fifty years or so. Before the laboratory experiments you mated according to your Darwin theory. The strongest and brightest of the species propagate each other."

"That's in animals," Dan protested.

"Even in medieval times, your people's strategy was to marry strength with beauty in order to produce the best for their kingdom. It's no different with any other planet. Each generation wants what is best for their descendants."

"Somehow I don't think that's the same as playing at gene-splicing."

"It's exactly the same," she corrected gently. "Only on a more primitive level."

"I see. To you we're some kind of chimp involved in a laboratory experiment," he stated dryly, not really believing it himself.

She looked surprised that he understood so quickly. "That's right."

"Are you kidding?" His voice rose with each syllable.

"No."

"Are you telling me you've used humans in experiments?"

"Yes. That's how I came to be."

"By mixing two races? Ovum and sperm? Splicing genes!"

"In the beginning, yes."

"How?"

"The usual way." Her chuckle was soft and light in the confines of the car.

"You mean to tell me some Herfronite came down here and screwed one of our own, had a baby and then sent that baby down here to repeat the procedure?"

"Yes." She frowned. "Primitive, but it worked. Now we use other means. It's easier."

"Lady, you're sick," he said disgustedly. "You need a hospital with padded walls and I need to be in the next room."

"Why?"

"Because I find it hard to believe that anyone would make love to some weirdo from outer space just because they needed the release."

"Why?"

"Because it's disgusting, that's why!"

She turned her head and stared, her big brown eyes focusing on him as if he were under a microscope. His hands clenched on the wheel. As hard as he tried to fight it, a heat slowly spread through his groin, growing, producing that heavy feeling that came just before one hell of an erection. Then he had that, too.

Only his whole body wasn't aroused; those feelings were localized in his groin.

"Stop it," he gritted through his teeth, and immediately the pressure began to ease.

Kendra leaned back, closing her eyes as if she was tired.

They sailed through Castroville without slowing down.

Kendra's eyes were still closed, her head leaning back. But he knew she wasn't asleep, just weary. Had the mind controlling, body controlling she had just done made her tired? If that was the case, he should make her even more tired. *What for?* he asked himself. There was nothing he could do except drop her by the side of the road and run. But something deep inside told him that if he found the answers to *his* Kendra's problems, he would begin to understand the change in their life together.

If what this woman said was true, his Kendra hadn't walked in front of that car on purpose. It had really been an accident, just as Ed had said. At least that was something. "She wanted a baby. She wanted to be a mother. After we lost the first one...we'd tried for so long." He took a deep breath. "You're crazy and I'm even crazier for listening to you. You're a figment of my imagination, and this is something I dreamed up because I don't want to believe that Kendra's dead. It's a defense mechanism."

"Believe what you will, I speak the truth."

The late-afternoon sun slanted into Kendra's side of the vehicle and she averted her face from its rays, curling into a ball on the seat and turning her back toward the heat.

"Kendra?"

"Yes?"

"But why? I was always there for her! Always!" After Hannah died, he'd tried to reach out to Kendra, but she had cut him out of her life, eliminating any need for the closeness or tenderness that he offered. Soon, she'd eliminated the need to even converse with him. He'd missed the touching, the stroking, the meeting of minds. He'd missed it so much it became a constant ache.

"She was always afraid to get pregnant again."

"What the hell is that supposed to mean?"

"She felt you had so much to keep you occupied and busy with your career. When you were home, she was afraid you would try to get her pregnant and then she'd have to go through another death. She was terrified of that. So she turned off the need for your touch, your presence. But your mind was elsewhere. Until bedtime. Then you added the pressure of sex— not the relief of touching without demand."

He felt the defense mechanism he had used for so long rise to protect him. "She never told me she didn't want sex."

"She also hated her fear of pregnancy and tried to fight against it. It was just too hard for her to win. She wasn't strong, Dan."

"That's not true. She did all kinds of things that only a strong person could do. When I was out of town, she was on her own, taking care of bills, repairmen, everything."

Kendra's eyebrows rose. "She followed a budget, cleaned house between the maid's weekly visits, put checks in envelopes and kept your clothing clean. Did she run out of money? Not have the best appliances? Where was the stress?"

"She was alone."

Kendra nodded. "She was lonely. That's not the same and isn't necessarily stress."

Kendra had been his breath, his life. And she was gone. He had loved her with all his heart. He'd have done anything he could to make her happy; he just hadn't known what else to do. His breath caught in his throat. "I tried."

"I know."

His fist slammed against the steering wheel. "Every year we took off like this to Big Bend! I tried to make it as romantic as I could. Just the two of us, dammit! Every year!"

"And she loved it. There was nothing to take away your attention. You focused on her."

"Then why did she put a stop to the trips?"

"For that same reason. She was afraid you would learn of her fears. She didn't think she'd make it through another death, Dan. As much as she loved you, she was frightened of you. She called off the trips and finally called off the marriage."

Dan remembered now. He'd come home from New York and begun talking about what they would need to pack for the anniversary trip to Big Bend. The more he talked the quieter she became. That night he had tried to draw her into his arms, but she had pleaded illness. Acting like a spoiled child and with a dramatically heavy sigh, he'd turned over and fallen immediately to sleep. Without touching, without cuddling.

The next morning she had left for her parents' home. He didn't know until he returned home to find a note and an empty apartment. She'd left for good. Her good. His good.

Damn!

First had come anger. How dared she leave him like that! Then had come fear. Would she return? Should he accept her back? And if he did, would he do so grudgingly, generously or thoughtfully?

But after a phone call to her parents, confusion had set in. Upon entering her parents' door she had collapsed and they couldn't stop the flow of tears. After several hours, they had taken her to the doctor's office. From there she was admitted to a psychiatric ward. Ed and Margaret had kept him informed after that.

Why hadn't he seen it coming? Maybe if he'd known, he could have fended it off. Stopped the downward spiral. Gotten her help. Done something!

Six months later she went to live with her parents, and he was only allowed limited visitation. Every time he saw her she seemed more distant. Each time, he felt the chasm widen between them and panicked at the thought of never having Kendra in his life. He begged her to come home. She said no. He demanded she return to him. She said no.

After two years of this, he'd made up his mind that if she said no during the next visit—this visit—he would accept it. He'd take the job in Israel, and try to begin a new life.

Dan had never been given an explanation for Kendra's leaving before. He'd dissected his marriage from beginning to end, but had found no answers.

Now he knew.

Assuming, of course, that he was sane; that the strange woman who resembled Kendra was really seated next to him.

And that *this* Kendra was right about *his* Kendra.

2

FLAT ARID LAND turned bumpy with brush and trees, like a scruffy three-day-old beard on the face of Earth. Dan used to tell his wife that when God decided to change the scenery He hadn't wanted to shock his children with anything too drastic, so he created the high desert.

He drove straight through the small town of Brackettville. Because of the terrain, it was the site of many Western movies, including *The Alamo*. Dan continued toward Del Rio. His hands were firmly on the wheel, his feet leaden on the pedals. But his mind was occupied with everything *but* the act of driving.

Kendra slept.

Soon, signs of civilization appeared, telling him he wasn't far from the town he'd chosen to spend the night. He passed the main entrance to a military air base, slowing down as the traffic became congested.

"Kendra, wake up," he said softly, almost afraid to have her alert. So much had buzzed through his mind since he'd picked her up that there had been no time to digest it. Perhaps when she stretched and awak-

ened, she would turn into an ordinary hitchhiker.
Perhaps....

The young woman who looked so much like his
wife straightened her spine and stretched her hands
out in front of her, nearly touching him. Although she
looked totally relaxed, she also seemed instantly alert.
"Umm," she murmured, glancing around the small
town before allowing her large brown eyes to settle on
him inquisitively. "So this is where we're stopping for
food?"

"Yes."

"At that lovely restaurant? The one with the car in
the lobby?"

He glanced at her before focusing on the road again.
"How did you know?"

She pulled her midnight-dark mane of hair together and finger combed it back over her shoulders.
"I saw it when you thought of it."

He wasn't dreaming. She was still a nut case.

She waited for a response, but he gave his complete
attention to the twisting road leading toward Amistad Dam. "Are you not going to formulate thoughts
anymore?"

"Yes." His answer was short and succinct.

"Will you allow me to read them?"

"I don't see how I can stop you." His voice was bitter with futility. He wasn't sure his frustration was
with her as much as it was with trying to deal with all
the emotions that were flooding him.

"Oh, that's easy." She swung her legs to the floorboards and stretched them out. They were tanned, long, supple.... "Think nonemotionally."

"And you can't read them?"

"Not easily." Her brow furrowed. "I've noticed that my ability to *malk* with my own kind has become a problem since I first came here. I've been trying to figure it out, but came up with too many possibilities. Perhaps the reason we don't allow our people to stay here longer is that we lose that which makes us different from you."

"By different you mean superior?"

She shrugged. "If you wish."

"What is your race like?"

"Compared to your race, we are a quiet people. We work together on everything to accomplish the ultimate achievement, and we usually succeed in our endeavors."

"But you're part human."

"Not the part that counts." It was a denial of anything human. "We are maintaining the Herfronite mind."

She acted as if there was no room for error, but life had taught Dan there was always a mistake here and there. "Then why are your powers being reduced?"

She frowned again. "I don't know, but we were warned that this might happen. Besides, it only seems to be lessened with those we work with. I can't seem to locate those who came with me, but I am fine with humans."

"'We' being *all* Herfronites or just third-generation ones?"

"We weren't told. The Kaus, the second generation, were sent here for the same purpose, but there were problems with them and several died or went insane from the pressure here before returning to Herfron."

"What is home like?"

"Similar to your east Texas, except our tall growths are not trees but spores and molds. Our food supply is vast."

"The atmosphere is warm?"

"It is cool. Our cities are temperature controlled because we—especially the Kaus and the Mais—have a tendency to chill faster than the original ones."

"Are there many originals left?"

She looked surprised. "Of course. They are our leaders, our minds, our lives."

"Sounds like a taste of George Orwell." Dan pulled into the restaurant parking lot and slid into a marked space by the door. Turning off the ignition, he stared at her. "Everything you say could be real or it could all be a figment of my imagination."

Her grin was positively impish. "You're right. It could be either."

Twilight shadows hid most of her face. *Which is it?* he wondered.

Real, she answered directly into his mind. *As real as you are.*

Dan closed his eyes and gulped back his fear. "Let's go," he growled. Stepping from the Jeep, he waited for her to alight, then took her arm. Busying himself with the ordinary, he decided, would give him time to absorb the extraordinary. He prayed he could do so. She calmly walked with him into the restaurant, sat down and ordered. At least she wasn't going to embarrass him by doing something . . . alien.

Kendra ordered a large salad and ate it with gusto while downing several glasses of iced tea. "Delicious," she announced when she placed her napkin next to her empty plate.

Dan stared down at his giant half-eaten hamburger, then pushed it aside. He'd lost his appetite.

"If you let yourself, you'll find it very tasty," she said gently.

"How would you know? Have you eaten here before?" He realized he sounded belligerent, but he didn't know how else to act. Everything was out of his control and he didn't have a clue how to regain command of the situation.

"No, but other humans in this restaurant think so. I only eat what you call vegetables."

"Then don't push what you haven't tried."

"I'm sorry."

Reaching for his wallet, he threw some bills down on the table and stood. "Let's get out of here." He left the restaurant without looking back at the woman who had stared up at him with large brown eyes. She brought out so many conflicting emotions in him he could hardly deal with walking back to the truck, let alone solving relationship problems with a dead wife. Nevertheless, he was afraid that she wouldn't follow him. He was also just as afraid that she would.

And she did follow him.

Just five miles up the road, Dan pulled into a hotel. More like a lodge, it sat smack on the edge of Amistad Dam, a large body of water caught between Mexico and the United States. The Rio Grande and the Pecos river had been pooled and dammed to form a huge, crystal clear lake. Retained as a wilderness, the area had become a boating-and-fishing resort to hundreds. Amistad was a success to all but the hungry land developers. They would have preferred more people, more homes, more resorts, more commercialism.

"We'll spend the night here," Dan told her.

"All right. What time are you planning to leave in the morning?"

"Early. Why?"

"I want to see what our first Herfronite space travelers looked like. I've seen the tapes, but the real thing must be different."

"How?" he demanded, standing next to the Jeep door as she stepped out and joined him on the raised sidewalk.

She motioned vaguely toward the water. "There are pictures in some caves in one of the tall cliffs."

He glanced at the sky. Twilight was turning quickly to night. "I'll go with you in the morning," he said.

"That's not necessary. I can find my way to Del Rio."

"I've taken you this far and we haven't killed each other yet. I'll take you the rest of the way."

She nodded and he turned away, unwilling to think of anything more than finishing this trip. Soon he'd be rafting on the river and she'd be . . . gone. Wherever the hell "gone" was supposed to be.

They walked into the orderly quiet of a small, not-quite-shabby lobby and he signed them both into one room. Without knowing why, he was suddenly afraid of losing contact with her.

He wrote his fear off as being the last link to Kendra—the woman he had lived with and loved for more years than he could count. The woman he hadn't known at all until today, if the alien beside him could be believed.

The worst part was that he *did* believe her.

The hotel room was cool. The closed blinds darkened the room completely and only a sole hanging lamp shed dim light through the large interior. Twin beds dressed in spreads that looked like 1970s Colonial had headboards bolted against the wall. Dan closed the door and leaned against it. He was exhausted from the events of the day, but even more frightened of tomorrow.

Kendra stood by the bathroom, her large purse still slung over her shoulder. Her hand tightened on the doorjamb as she gave a sad smile. "Why would I kill you, Dan?" she asked softly, reading his mind again.

Straightening, he faced her, hands on his hips. "You tell me."

"Herfronites don't believe in killing. Besides, I can wipe out your memories as easily as I can give them. See?" She held out her hands, palms up. "There is no need for killing. You're taking me where I must go. I'll try to help you over the loss of your wife and I've kept my promise to her. We're even."

It almost sounded fair, but hell, what did he know? He was talking to an alien! "How much do you know about Kendra?"

"Concerning your relationship with her?"

Afraid to speak for fear his voice would crack, he nodded.

"Just about everything. She didn't think of much else these past six months. I know less about her childhood than I do about your life with her. She was readying herself for your homecoming."

He closed his eyes as the pain of her words hit him like sharp nails biting into his skin. If his Kendra had lived, his homecoming would have been different this time. They could have been together and he would have been in her arms tonight, feeling secure in love and safe from loneliness....

The bathroom door clicked quietly and he knew she'd left him alone. Still he stood there, attempting to recuperate from the outpouring of facts and emotions that had deluged him all day.

Be patient. I'll help. Her message rang in his head and he realized that even through closed doors, she could speak to him.

Finally Dan moved. He set his overnighter on the chair and unzipped it. *Do regular things and life will be regular.*

Sleep was a long time in coming. The lengthy shower, the nightcap of brandy from his flask, the promise of answers in the morning—none of those worked to soothe his tensed nerves or frantic thoughts. Eyes wide open, he lay in bed, hands behind his head, and stared at the ceiling.

Once, he felt her entering his thoughts with a tranquillizing gentleness. "Stop that," he ordered harshly. The comforting sensations stopped. But her "magic" had helped.

Finally, he went to sleep.

"OVER THERE!" Kendra pointed, shouting above the roar of the boat motor, and he followed her directions and steered toward the canyon wall. There was an opening—a cove with sheer cliffs running upward like a block of stone before a master chiseler, waiting to be formed into something even more grand. She sat in the front of the boat, her dark hair whipping in the breeze like a gorgeous flag of honor.

Mexico was on Dan's right and the United States on his left as he guided the rented boat toward a floating dock. He looked out over the water, realizing for the first time that, with the exception of a lone Mexican fisherman in a homemade boat on the far side of the lake, they were alone.

"Tie up here," she ordered. Ever since last night when he'd been so sharp with her, she had only spoken to him aloud, and even then, she hadn't said much. Yesterday, she had shown glimmers of humor, of emotion. Of life. Now she was an alien again, intent on seeing the proof of her people's past. He hated to admit that he missed the woman she was when they met.

He did as she asked, then stepped onto the pier and held out his hand. Placing hers trustingly in his, she jumped to the floating dock, staring unblinkingly at him all the while.

He couldn't help but ask, "What are you thinking?"

"That you're sad, and I'm feeling that sadness, too. It's unusual." She was just as blunt as she had been yesterday. Didn't she know how to lie?

She tilted her head and a mischievous glint shone in her eyes. "No. At least, not very well." She gave a brilliant smile that he felt all the way to his toes. Her hand, pliant and soft, was still in his. "When others can read your mind you might as well tell the truth. Otherwise you spend time and energy building a wall around your thoughts. When others feel it, they know you are lying."

Her hand was warm, her fingers lax until she gave a light squeeze that heated more than his hand. He dropped it quickly. Forcing himself to turn from her, he stared at the overgrown path leading up the face of the cliff. "Where to now?"

"Right up there. Follow me." She scrambled like a crab, finding footholds as she went. Halfway up she stopped to laugh melodically, throwing her arms in the air to embrace the warming sun. Her laugh was a free, low-toned sound that seemed to rustle like the wind around them.

"What?" he asked, frowning. He glanced around to see if he had missed something.

"Nothing." She looked down over her shoulder at him. "It's just a beautiful day."

"Move it," he ordered gruffly.

She did.

Reaching a ledge more than three-quarters of the way up the steep wall of stone, she turned and offered him her hand. He ignored it, pulling himself up by hanging on to a bush. He wasn't ready to touch her again. Whenever that happened, the heat between them seemed too intense. If she wasn't really Kendra, it was a wrong feeling.

I'm sorry you think that way.

"Stay out of my mind!" He glared at her.

A smile tugged at her mouth—a mouth the color of peach blossoms. "Yes, sir!" She accompanied the words with a smart salute.

He couldn't help smiling back.

As Kendra walked along the ledge he followed close behind. They finally stopped in front of a chain link fence behind which was a shallowly scooped-out section of the cliff; both were as high as a two-story building.

"Behold," she said, sweeping her hand out with a flourish. "Your ancestors and mine. I believe your people call them pictographs."

The wall was covered with drawings too numerous to see all at once—designs of every description in yellow and red ochre paint. The first drawing to catch his eye was an enormous ruby-colored panther, with a tail curling around its body like a powerful whip. Although the red paint had faded somewhat, the color was still bright enough to capture the imagination. The huge "cat" measured at least seven or eight feet wide and half that high. The tail was so long it wrapped around the panther's underside as if to underline or emphasize what the artist couldn't put into words.

Now that the first shock was over, Dan realized that the drawings all harmonized with one another, evoking sheer pleasure in the viewer. Like today's big bill-

boards advertising products for the times, the pictures
here told of their times, too. Ancient man, in his need
to communicate, wasn't too different from modern
man.

Fascinated, he studied each one—the smaller pictographs first. Some were stick figures, others more
filled out and detailed; all were alive with a vibrancy
that transported them out of history and right into the
present. Suddenly he stopped, as his gaze fixed on one
particular drawing to the left of the panther.

What it depicted was undeniable: in the midst of
other, more typical Native American-type drawings,
stood a spaceman—complete with suit and helmet.

"Look to the right." She spoke quietly, just loud
enough to gain his attention without startling him.

He did as he was told. Next to the spaceman stood
a crude version of a flying saucer. Stunned, he said the
first thing that came to his mind: "I don't believe it."

Kendra's chuckle was low, sweet and totally ignored. "If you hadn't met me, you'd look at the drawings and smile, chalking it up to an ancient artist's
fantastic imagination."

Knowing she was probably right, he still denied it.
"You don't know that."

"Yes, I do. Thousands of people have already stood
in this exact place. None—or very few—had any
proof that men from outer space were visitors before
their own birth. To them it was fantasy. To you it's a

reality you choose to deny because you can't quite accept me as an alien. At least, not yet."

"And you think I will later?" He turned, searching her brown eyes, translucent skin and slim neck for some sign of the alien being she claimed to be.

He found nothing. She was a beautiful woman.

"I think your logical mind has already accepted it. It did almost as soon as you met me. But your emotions stand in the way. Just as they do with all humans."

"And your people aren't emotional?" He was angry but he didn't know why or with whom. He wasn't even sure why he was denying her statement. Deep down, he knew she was probably right.

As Kendra thought about it a moment, her head tilted to the side, reminding him so much of his Kendra....

"We are, but not at the level your people are. We work together on everything, and the parameters of behavior and emotions are quite concrete in our society. Our rules and laws—social and economic—are written in stone, and it is easier because giving our word commands the same respect as offering money." She smiled. "It's much easier when you know what is acceptable behavior, and that anything outside that parameter means being harshly ostracized."

He looked back at the images drawn on the cave wall some seven thousand or more years ago. Had the Native American artist taken the subject of his painting for granted because he and his people had accepted the existence of such strange creatures?

"Be at peace," she said softly, resting her hand on his arm.

Dan felt the heat of her touch—and resented it. "My God, you people are coming down here individually and collectively, probably changing the course of history, and you're telling me to be at peace? One of us is crazy, lady, and I'm not sure it's me!" Pulling his arm away, he left her and strode to the side of the cliff to begin the descent back to the rented boat below.

A few moments later, she followed. He knew, because he sensed her presence as surely as he felt the gravel beneath his feet. He forced his mind blank. He couldn't cope with more mind probing from this strange woman.

He'd been shaken to his roots at seeing seven-thousand-year-old pictographs that showed spacemen near the isolated Big Bend area. Especially after meeting a woman who had absorbed his wife's memories—or so she claimed.

For reasons he didn't delve into, he waited for her at the boat. It would have been so easy to take off and leave the alien there, but it wouldn't have answered any of the thousand questions that swirled in his brain.

As soon as Kendra sat down in the bow of the boat, Dan headed toward open water.

It was time to go to Big Bend. Meanwhile, he needed to sort out his questions and ask them in a logical manner. He couldn't remain swamped in emotions. As she had commented earlier, humans were emotional. If he had to deal with her to gain the answers, he'd better deal on her level.

They were back on the highway to Lajitas immediately after returning the rental boat and checking out of the lodge. He'd been silent for over an hour as they drove through barren land and toward the mountains ahead.

"Damn," she muttered, staring at her finger.

"What's wrong?" While he'd been wrapped in thought, he'd forgotten she was sitting right next to him.

"I broke a nail."

He looked at her, then down at her hand and up again. "More logical, less emotional? It seems your genetic splicing failed to take into account that human emotions are heightened as their genes become stronger."

She grinned.

He matched it.

She laughed and he joined in. "I think you're right," she admitted. "On my planet we have short, suitable-for-work nails. No one would dream of having anything longer. But here, long nails are the 'in' thing for women," she stated ruefully. "I actually felt *angry* over a broken nail!

"You know," she began, then hesitated, her brow furrowed in a frown. It dawned on him that she was always doing that—and it was as unlike his Kendra as could be. His Kendra always spoke before she thought.

"From what I've seen," she continued, "women look the most vulnerable on the outside but are very strong centered on the inside. They're quicker to read emotions and minds than men."

He wasn't going to tell her how right she was. "And what are your observations about men?"

"Just the opposite. Men seem very strong on the outside and so very insecure on the inside. They seem afraid to read their own emotions or anyone else's. They're more comfortable with surface reactions."

"You and three hundred psychologists agree," he muttered.

She shrugged. "Probably. Herfronites are able to read both telepathic and body signals. It's a way of life for us, necessary for our continued growth."

"If Herfronites are so great, then why are they mating with poor dumb humans?"

She frowned. "I didn't say you were dumb. And the reason is simple. We are using your physical strength. We don't have that in our race. In blending the best assets of both species, we hope to join the best of both attributes."

"Don't you realize you're more human than Herfronite?" His voice held a challenge.

She smiled at him as if he were a small child making simple demands. But her looks and their effect on him were anything but childlike.

"In your country you have blacks who have a mixture of ancestors. But you continue to call them black, even if they're only one-eighth of that race. I'm only a third-generation Herfronite. One human/one Herfronite-in-two generation. Our scientists have also tried to retain our working ability and mental capacity, making changes only in the body. Ergo I am far more Herfronite than most of your blacks are black."

"You're crazy," he said for lack of anything else to say. No matter how stupid it sounded, she was absolutely right. "Besides, I'm supposed to believe that you're a Herfronite because I've seen a cave drawing of someone or something you claim is an ancestor. I think you're a good hypnotist."

"You think I can read your mind that easily?"

Dan nodded, but he wasn't sure what he was saying yes to. "I just lost my wife and I'm in a weakened state. It's possible this whole thing is going on in my head, and you're either not here at all or I picked you up on the highway and I'm really helping you escape from some crazy farm!"

She turned in her seat, facing him once more. Her heart-shaped face was earnest in her desire to understand. "If I could, I would show you our ship, but I made a promise to my race that I would never do that."

His heart tripped over itself. "Who would know?"

"You would. I would. Soon, other Herfronites would." She shook her head and her silky hard hair bounced in the sunlight just like Kendra's used to, spitting threads of copper through the satiny coal. "It's impossible. My word is all I have and it is important enough to live or die for."

Still he pressed. "You weren't supposed to promise anything to Kendra, but you did."

"That was the only way I could help her," she argued, trying to be logical. "I will explain that to my superiors and I am sure they will understand."

"Where is your ship?"

"Near the river."

"Where?"

She grinned, teasing him instead of getting angry about his persistence. "If I told you, then my word would be broken. It would be the same as leading you there, don't you think?"

"No. I think I could find it myself and then no one could blame you."

"But I would still *know*. That means that my superiors would know."

"How are you getting there?"

Kendra shrugged. "Walking."

"From Lajitas? That's got to be quite a walk in any direction. American side or Mexican?"

"American. I was planning to have you drop me off in Big Bend National Park."

"I'll take you where you want to go." Dan ran a hand through his hair. "I don't think I'll sleep well unless I believe you're safe from whatever harm might be out there." He took a good look at her again. "And with your looks, hell knows what surprises might be in store for you."

"There aren't that many people in the park."

"There are at the lodge. And there are lots of drop-outs who live in caves, cabins and tents in that lonely stretch of country. They don't like people and they're not sure about animals." He saw her frown as she digested this information, and pressed his point. "It might be easier to get to your ship from water."

Her brows lifted. "*Now* who's doing the mind reading?"

"I was guessing." He didn't bother to tell her that more flying saucers were spotted out there and in New Mexico every year than anywhere else.

"Well, the ship is close, but I don't swim."

"I do. And I'm going by raft down the Rio Grande."

She leaned forward and her dark hair draped over her shoulder like a midnight-colored curtain. "You wouldn't mind taking me with you?"

"Not at all."

"I will not let you see the ship." Her voice held a warning.

"I understand."

Kendra leaned back, a satisfied smile on her face. "This would be a wonderful opportunity for our memory tapes." She hesitated, then nodded her head as if agreeing to a discussion inside her head. "Yes. If you are going rafting, I'll go with you."

"Great." He felt as if he'd pulled off a coup. If he got close, then he'd see the damned thing. Once and for all, he'd know the truth about the woman sitting next to him.

She caught his attention by taking a deep breath. "I have to get there anyway, so I might as well go by water as by land. This experience would definitely help our people."

"Your people, not mine."

Kendra leaned back and was silent several long minutes. He was dying to insist on knowing her thoughts, but he was equally afraid to break into her reverie. Besides, their whole relationship was becoming so fascinating, he didn't want it to end. Not yet. His engineer's mind found everything she said logical, if weird.

"I'm surprised," she finally murmured. "But I find that I want you to believe me for my sake as well as for your wife's. You see, I made a promise to her that I would let you know her feelings for you. If you don't believe me completely now, then, when I wipe out your memory of me you might not believe your memories of her. That would defeat my promise."

"And why do you want me to believe you for your sake?"

She tilted her head and stared at him, her brow etched in puzzlement. "I'm not sure I know yet. Interesting. At home I would have no problem being believed. No one would dare lie. Here it's even done in the context of manners, so one won't hurt another's feelings. It's a strange concept, but one that seems to work for humans."

"So you're proving your word is your bond."

"Something like that."

Dan was pleased she'd agreed—he couldn't lose this woman just yet.

3

THE SMALL TOWN of Lajitas in far-west Texas was just
seventeen miles from Terlingua, a onetime mining
town and much-promoted chili capital of the Southwest. A few trees grew by the adobe-walled building
that squatted on the banks of the Rio Grande. The
thick-walled store was all that was left of the turn-of-
the-century trading post.

Some two hundred people lived in or around Lajitas. Most of them worked for one of the river-raft
companies or at the hotel/restaurant that was a mini-
vacation spot and stop-off for those who traversed the
river.

Dan nosed the Jeep toward the town boardwalk, a
long wooden structure that ran the length of six or
seven shops made to look like something from the Old
West.

"What are you doing?" Kendra asked, uncurling her
legs.

Reaching across her lap, Dan punched the glove
compartment button, then grabbed a credit card
holder. "Can't you read my mind?"

"No." She sounded almost petulant. "You've been blocking me since we left Del Rio."

He raised a skeptical brow. "I didn't know it was that easy."

"Only because I don't probe hard."

"There are levels of probing?" He flipped through several credit cards, then extracted one. "I'm surprised you haven't tried harder."

"It is not a Herfronite's way to hurt someone, and probing hard could do that."

"According to what you've said so far, you've broken other rules. Why not break this one, too? After all, it's just a lowly human's mind you're playing with, not a lofty Herfronite's."

She touched his arm, stopping him from moving out of the truck. "Please, let us be friends. We have only a short time together. Let's spend it pleasantly."

He let out a heavy sigh, reluctant to admit she was right. He'd been angry, mean and willing to attack anyone ever since he'd learned the devastating news of Kendra's death. It might as well end now. He could at least be civil until he got a few more answers to some very intriguing questions. "Peace," he finally said.

She smiled. "Peace."

He didn't like the fact that she looked beautiful when she smiled. He didn't like it one bit. If it was possible, she was more fascinating than he remembered the original Kendra to be. She was also far more open and quick to speak. He felt guilty for making the comparison. This whole set of circumstances was crazy.

Dan reached for the door handle, then stopped and stared at her a moment. "Would you like to spend the night here or on the river?" he found himself asking.

She answered immediately. "On the river."

"I'll make the arrangements," he said, glancing at his watch. "But we won't have much time on the water before we have to set up camp. It's almost four o'clock now."

"We'll do it." She spoke confidently, as if she knew something he didn't. He looked at her, then realized that she was only echoing his own wishes.

"Be right back," he promised, a smile in his voice. He'd been so quick to anger or become frustrated that he had forgotten to read her own, very sensual, body language. She seemed at ease and casual with him. Open. Not bad for an alien.

KENDRA SAT QUIETLY, waiting for Dan to return from the rafting company's office. She remained utterly still, her mind stretching, trying to reach to any of her kind in the area. There should be several Herfronites here.

It was odd that in the one week she had spent in San Antonio she had learned so much about Dan's race. Her training hadn't taught what human beings were really like. Though equally kind and cruel to one another, humans were not quite the barbarians she had been taught they would be.

Far more of them had psychic abilities than she would have imagined—including Dan. And most of these, it seemed, preferred not to allow their abilities free rein. Very odd.

She stilled her mind again and tried once more to touch one of her kind. A small shimmer of thought came her way, then disappeared. She tried to reach out for it, but to no avail. What had gone wrong?

She played over the accumulated memories of the past week, taking each day at a time and recalling the strength and weakness of her telepathic powers at the start and end of each day. In the beginning she had *malked* with many who had made the trip from Herfron with her. Then, they had slowly drifted away. One or two had refused to answer or *malk* at all, and had disappeared completely. She'd thought it was her fault. Could she have been wrong? Could *their* powers have dwindled?

She frowned, biting her lip just as Kendra did. Now that she was examining it, her mind-reading powers had become weaker with each passing day. Was she the only one having this reaction? Or had her fellow travelers become weaker, too?

She remembered the warnings that had been drummed into her. *Always obey every rule set forth. If one Herfronite strays from the rules, tell another immediately.* And most important: *Never stay on*

Earth longer than one week, unless connected to a Guardian. Had she used up too much energy in collecting Kendra's thoughts? She didn't know. Perhaps she would find out when she met up with some of the others at the spaceship in the next two days.

A sharp stab of regret filled her at the thought of leaving Earth. She had become immersed in the culture—a very human and not-very-Herfronite thing to do. And she had truly gotten emotionally involved with just one person—Dan.

She had broken rules she never should have, and made excuses for breaking them—excuses like hoping that her own people would be able to use the information. Now it almost seemed disloyal to admit that, even to herself. It was most unlike her. Perhaps the old Kendra was more of a rebel than she'd thought....

She wasn't always sure which emotions were Kendra's and which ones were her own. What she felt for Dan was tenderness, sympathy and a kind of vulnerability to him; a very human set of emotions. And there was something else—something very strong but foreign to her; something she couldn't yet put a name to.

Returning to the truck, Dan opened the door and slipped into the driver's seat. He stared at her with blue eyes that were like steel needles that could pierce through her to see the thousands of small problems she saw ahead. "Are you okay?"

She nodded.

He backed the truck out of its parking space and headed across the street to a large metal building. "I'm getting the raft blown up here and then we'll leave. These guys will pick up my Jeep and take it to the end point for me."

She nodded again as if she understood.

It was another fifteen minutes before they were on the empty, two-lane highway headed north. Their rubber raft was tied to the top of the truck, fresh ice was packed in the food chest and there was an empty rubber bag in the back seat. Dan had explained that it was to hold their clothing and whatever else they didn't want to get wet.

The old Kendra's thoughts and memories over the past six months hadn't dwelled on the working part of their annual trips down the Rio Grande. Only the funny, teasing, loving memories had been relived and savored. Odd snatches of dialogue, intimate looks that communicated without words, touches that brought strong emotions. Memories that had little to do with sex and everything to do with that elusive emotion humans called love.

The new Kendra shook her head in wonder. Two days ago she'd been amazed that Dan's wife could have reveled in those feelings and not paid the slightest attention to where she was going when she stepped off that curb.

Now that she was beginning to experience those same emotions herself, she understood. She searched her own memories and thoughts, and came to the same conclusion she had reached earlier: she was quite sure that her own emotions were similar to the old Kendra's. And with a yearning that was palpable, she wanted Dan to say, to do, to feel the things the old Kendra had memories of. Only she wanted him to do it with *her*.

This frightened her.

Dan slowed down, stopped, then backed into a break in the low desert shrubbery. From behind her, Kendra could here the dull roar of rushing water and she tensed. Although they had water on their planet, most of her race considered it an "environmental" threat. The ground on their planet that wasn't cultivated did not readily absorb water. Instead, they experienced raging floods. Herfronites were heavy and ploddingly slow. They were terrible swimmers. Just the sound of rushing water was enough to warn a Herfronite to start moving toward higher ground.

Dan glanced over at her, noting her reaction. "We're here. You're hearing the river rapids."

"I thought so," she muttered, holding on to the door as he eased the truck backward, parked it in a scrub-shaded area at the water's edge and stepped out, all in one fluid motion.

It took several seconds for Kendra to react, and when she did it was with jerky motions. She was still a little frightened by the sound of water, but she also knew that she was only holding on to a fear with no basis for it.

"Can I help?" she asked, as she finally went to the back of the truck where Dan was unloading the equipment and securing it in the rubber raft he had already set at the water's edge.

"Just sit tight until I'm through," he barked, quickly continuing his task.

"I'm able to lift and tote, you know."

That stopped him. His eyes narrowed on her a moment, then rolled down her slim form and back up, hesitating only a split second longer at the fullness of her T-shirt. She felt a flush begin at her neck, but then descend to fill her breasts with a tightness she was unfamiliar with. He resumed his packing. "It's my equipment, I'll do it."

She stood, hands on her hips as she watched him, biting her lip to avoid telling him off. Within a matter of minutes everything was packed except the contents of his suitcase. He reached for the case, snapped open the top and grabbed the rubber bag next to it. Unceremoniously, he dumped the contents into the bottom of the rubber bag.

Then he finally looked at her. "Where are your clothes?"

"In the back."

"Get them."

She did. She only had one change of clothes and two sets of underwear. She hadn't needed more for a week on planet Earth. At least she hadn't thought she would.

He looked at the contents. "This is it?"

She nodded, her own gaze daring him to comment further. It had been a very long week and she only recently found that she'd inherited a temper. Fury must have been something Dan could sense, because he took one look at her and said nothing.

She let out her breath in a slow, measured sigh. It was a full minute before she realized she had read him in the human way instead of the Herfronite way: body language versus *malking*.

It was yet another frightening realization of the changes she was undergoing.

Two young men in a pickup pulled in front of Dan's Jeep. As one of them stepped from the passenger seat, Dan gave a grin and tossed them his keys. "Thanks, guys, I'll look downriver right after Santa Elena Canyon."

"Right," the one said and slid into Dan's driver's seat. Two minutes later, both the Jeep and the pickup were gone.

Dan visually checked over the boat, tugged on a bungee cord that held one of the coolers and gave a satisfied grunt. "Get in," he ordered, nodding his head toward the rubber raft.

She eyed what looked like a very flimsy craft—especially compared to the rapids that began just fifteen feet away. "Where do I sit?"

"In the bow. The narrowest end."

Trusting in Dan because she had no choice, she climbed over the side and sat down on the cooler strapped there. The raft was filled with all sorts of things. Again, she searched Kendra's memory banks. Paddles, four. Two coolers. Three life vests in a glaring orange. A hard-formed container she knew was filled with a sleeping bag and ground pad along with a few other personal necessities. Toilet paper, matches, a small spade, two gallons of drinking water.

"Put on a life vest," Dan said as he reached for one himself.

Grateful that it was there, she reached for it and undid the straps—but not silently. "Stop ordering me."

He looked up, surprised. Kendra had never told him off, even calmly.

He had the grace to look sheepish. "Sorry. I was thinking of something else."

She wasn't about to delve into his mind to find out what it was. She didn't trust her reactions, and hadn't since she had realized she was experiencing strong, new, human emotions. It wouldn't do to let him know her feelings, and he would certainly learn them if she tried to mingle their thoughts.

She slipped her arms through the life vest, watching him as he adjusted his, mimicking his actions until the fit felt snugly correct.

He gave the boat a shove away from shore. He was careful not to touch her as he reached for the oars and began to travel the main current of the river, which was now swirling all around them.

An almost-overwhelming sadness came over her. She had only two more days with Dan before she would leave him forever.

AS THE SOUND OF rushing water bounced off Colorado Canyon's stone walls, Dan felt himself relax. It was the first time since he'd returned that he knew what to do. Winding his way through the tall canyons was *real;* something that he could control and manage. Maneuvering the raft downriver was skillful habit. He determinedly ignored the femininely-slim back just two feet in front of him.

Kendra glanced at him over her shoulder, with a smile that was as soothing as the rushing sound of the water. "It's beautiful here, isn't it?" She looked slightly surprised, as if she hadn't expected to enjoy the trip. "Yes."

Her eyes locked with his and he felt the flow of empathy and communion from her. "You should live here instead of a big city. You're really a country boy at heart."

His eyes narrowed. Once more, he attacked rather than admit his intense attraction to her. "I thought you said you'd only been here a week. What the hell do you know about country boys?"

"We were all trained to be able to go anywhere on Earth. Then we were chosen for a particular terrain. My lot was the United States, then Texas, then narrowed to San Antonio."

The oars stopped their movement. "You mean you came to Earth with more of your kind?"

She nodded, her expression telling him she knew what was going to come next.

"How many?" His voice was hoarse.

"Twenty that I know about."

"All females?"

Her eyes dropped. "This time."

Then he asked the question that he'd wanted to ask for the past two days but hadn't had the nerve. Until now, it had been too much to contend with; too much to grasp all at once. But he couldn't hold it off any longer. "What are you here for? Don't give me a *general* idea. *Tell* me."

Kendra leaned back. "Did you talk to your wife this way?"

"What way?"

"Bossy."

"Yes," he replied. "And don't change the subject. What are you here for?"

"I can't," Kendra stated. "No wonder she had no confidence in her own decisions. You were so sure for her, that she didn't need to be sure for herself. With no practice, it would be harder to learn when you're older."

"She could have spoken up whenever she wanted to. You certainly do." The rapids had dissolved and the river had turned smooth; the undercurrent ran just beneath the surface water with a placid surety. "Tell me something about it or I'll drop you off here," he threatened, knowing there was no chance either one of them would believe that.

She confirmed it with her answer. "No."

But he couldn't leave it alone. "Are you trying to take over our planet? Is that it? You've run out of water or air or food sources and need ours to survive?"

Kendra swiveled her bottom on the ice chest and faced him. Their knees were almost touching. "We don't need any of that."

"Then what?" He knew his expression was just as confused as his thoughts, but he had to know.

"I can't tell you. But I will say that it won't hurt you or your people. You'll never miss what we want."

Dan was feeling venomous. He steered around the next bend, staring at the water as if reading it like the pages of a book. The bright orange ball of sun began its nightly routine of dropping below the top wall of the canyon, lengthening shadows into grotesque shapes.

He hated riddles. Straight answers to straight questions didn't seem like such a damn hard thing to ask from a woman—or from an alien—whatever. But he also knew he wasn't getting the answer now. Later, he promised himself, when she didn't have her guard up, he would pester her until he got the answer.

He glanced at his watch. It was time to find a campsite and set up for the night. He angled the boat to the Mexican side of the river where there was a high spot of green grass and cedar trees filled with wispy purple blossoms. It must have rained recently, for the desert was alive with fragrant blossoms of all colors.

"We'll camp here," he said, jumping into the ankle-high water and scraping the boat over the rocks.

Kendra helped unload the lightweight necessities, then watched Dan carefully as he trekked back and forth from the boat to the spot he'd designated as camp. He could feel her eyes, sense her light probing into his mind. But he'd learned a lot in the past two days. He cut out his personal thoughts by silently detailing each move he made.

The light touch of her hand on his arm stopped him. "Please, don't shut me out."

He felt as frustrated as she must. "What the hell do you care? You're not one of us. You're not even from this damn planet! And you won't tell me what you're doing here. For all I know, you're going to eradicate my race!"

"Don't be silly, you know I wouldn't do that or allow anyone else to do that. It's not the Herfronite way. I'm part of your race. Doesn't that count for something? I care for you. I've broken so many rules already I can hardly begin to count them. Bear with me while I straighten out my own thoughts. Then perhaps I can help you with yours."

"Help me how? By not answering simple questions?"

"I'll tell you about Kendra."

His anger left as quickly as it had surfaced, leaving only the sadness of futility behind. "I don't believe you."

She nodded, her dark hair twisting gently in the early-evening breeze. "I will. There's much you don't know, don't understand, but I'll explain it to you."

He dropped the rubber bag stuffed with sleeping gear on the ground. "Go ahead."

Licking her lips, she toured the area, nervousness apparent in every fiber of her being. "After we set up camp," she finally said.

With a look that told her what he thought of the idea, Dan picked up the rest of the gear and began setting up the small area he had designated as the campsite. He finished his unpacking, then unrolled the sleeping bags, placing them a foot apart. That was more than enough space to ensure they were sleeping separately. Last, he walked several hundred feet back from the water's edge and dug a hole. Next to it, he laid the Ziplock bag of toilet paper and matches.

Having nothing specific to do, Kendra gathered several pieces of deadwood, piling them next to one of the sleeping bags. Then she sat down and waited.

She didn't have to wait long. Dan returned and reached into one of the ice chests, pulling out a beer and two wrapped sandwiches. "I brought these for tonight. They're poor-boy sandwiches."

She accepted one of them, then stared dubiously at the meat. Dan sighed. "Look, I'll take the meat, you eat the cheese and bread. If you're still hungry, then grab an apple or pear. Both are in the chest."

Her relieved smile was unexpected and curled around his heart with a warmth that felt like a spring thaw. "Thank you," she said quietly.

Sitting cross-legged, she carefully began separating the meats from the cheese. Putting her sandwich aside, she handed Dan the luncheon meat. He took it and exchanged his cheese and lettuce with her.

"Tell me more about your people."

"What would you like to know?" she asked around a bite of her sandwich. "I thought I mentioned everything of interest."

"How long have you been visiting our planet?"

"Several thousand years."

"Why?"

She shrugged. "To visit. To teach. To learn."

"Do you visit other galaxies or is ours the only one so lucky?"

"We visit many galaxies. Each one seems to have at least one form of life. Some have hundreds. It varies."

"Why are you here? Why this planet? Why a third generation of whatever?" He asked the one question uppermost in his mind. "Why us?"

Kendra bit into the last of her sandwich and folded the wrap into a neat square. She watched him swallow the last bite of his and wad up the paper, then reach over and toss it into the plastic bag he had opened earlier. "I don't know. On my planet, I'm no more privileged about the big picture than you are.

"I'm not here to talk about my own planet, but to help you understand Kendra. I promised I would do that before I left. Don't you want to know about her?"

Dan leaned back and stretched out on the sleeping bag. Placing his hands behind his head, he stared at the sky that was now darkening from shimmering pastels to indigo blue. One star stood out: a star that Kendra—*his* Kendra—always looked for first. He wished he knew what star it was. "Yes."

He felt as if he was talking about someone other than his wife. He didn't know why or how to change it. Hell, he didn't even know if he *wanted* to change it! With this Kendra in front of him, he could almost pretend that his wife was still alive and with him. It was less painful that way. But it wasn't realistic. He knew he couldn't deny her death any longer. "What did she want me to know?"

"That she loved you so much, but until just before she died, she wasn't willing to fight for that love."

Her words hit him in the stomach like an unsuspecting gut-punch. "Then it wasn't a very strong love, was it?"

She looked at him as if admonishing him for his wrongful thoughts. "That was Kendra's reasoning all those years. She felt guilty because she couldn't open up that part of herself that would allow you to see just how scared she really was." Her head tilted to the side as she stared at him thoughtfully. "What an odd thing to cause guilt."

"You're telling me that she felt so guilty that eight years into our marriage she couldn't stand the pressure of her own guilt anymore, so she left me and had a nervous breakdown?" He snorted. "Are you sure you don't have a brother named Grimm?"

"No. Her guilt, misplaced as it was, began a pattern she never broke. It was her crutch."

"I don't believe this. She didn't love me enough. It's that simple." But he did believe. A small voice in the back of his mind told him she was right. Too many things added up. Memories he'd thought were long dead came back in brilliant, living color. He remembered the change that had come over her in their senior year of high school. He'd thought it was due to growing up, but he was wrong.

"No," he croaked again.

"She loved you too much and she was too weak.

"And the more you sympathized with her, the worse she became, finally screaming at you to leave her alone. She had wanted to die rather than face life without having the role of mother as an identity and not feeling quite brave enough to have another child and fight the odds again. Not long after, she had the breakdown, because she couldn't cope with losing the child she had prayed for."

"I don't believe you." His voice was so low it was a whisper. He closed his eyes, willing the darkness outside to invade him, make him blind to the reality of the missing puzzle pieces finally falling into place. It explained so much.

"Yes, you do. You choose to deny it. She loved you but she wasn't the person you thought she was. She'd decided to face you, and see if you two could try again. However, your Kendra also believed that she was no longer your priority, that you'd gone on with your life and didn't really need her. She felt you'd be asking for a divorce soon. Is that right?"

His Kendra. He would give his life to hold her again. He'd always believed his love would overcome all. His wife was right about his reaction. He was the one who couldn't read her, not the other way around.

Tears seeped from his closed eyes and trickled down the sides of his face. He didn't care. Now he knew her fears. And he saw his own mistakes. But could they ever have worked out their problems? Changed their very natures? Even if she'd returned to him, he doubted if it would have worked out between them.

A pain slashed through him so deep and so sharp it cut off his breath, stabbing through his gut. He clenched his teeth with the power of it.

"Oh, Dan, don't," she whispered, leaning over him and wiping away a trail of tears with her fingertip. "Don't," she repeated, her whisper-soft kiss replacing the wetness of his tears.

Eyes still closed with the pain, he reached for her, unable to stop himself in his overwhelming need for comfort.

She rested against him, her hands clinging to his shoulders. Her full breasts flattened against the hardness of his chest. She continued to kiss the side of his face with lips warm and supple. So sweet, so healing. . . .

"Kendra," he said through the lump in his throat. It was a cry for help. He didn't know whether he was talking to his Kendra and trying to deny their inability to stay together or if he was speaking to the new, stronger Kendra. "Be with me."

"Yes," she said. Her hand slipped between them, touching him through his cutoffs, showing him she knew what he meant.

He sobbed in relief. Kendra. His Kendra was in his arms again.

4

SOFT, SUPPLE BREASTS burned against his skin, firing his blood with promises of ecstasy and release.

He needed a chance to make it up to Kendra, to tell her how much he'd loved her, waited for her— No. He pulled away and leaned his head against hers. This wasn't *that* Kendra. This was another woman.

She drew back but Dan tightened his hold on her. "Don't go."

"I won't," she murmured. "I can't. This feels too pleasant to stop."

"Does that mean you *want* to continue?" he teased, more relaxed now that he knew she wasn't leaving him.

"Yes. Yes." Kendra's slim fingers sought and found his zipper. The sound of the rushing river was wiped out by the raucous sound of its release.

He sighed in relief. His Kendra's touch had always wiped away the tiredness of spirit he felt when he was away from her. Always.... Her hand surrounding hard flesh, her fingers closing to milk his very substance from him. A shiver raced up his spine like a shock wave, sending responses to other parts of him.

Her touch was so right, and he wanted badly to make her feel the same rush of emotions she was creating in him.

"Yes," he whispered, finding the malleable softness of her breast in his palm and flexing his fingers around the wonder of it. It felt different, yet the same. Once more, he recognized features unique to each of the two women. They were the same, yet different....

Slowly, hesitantly, her mind reached toward him, touched the parameters of his. Tendrils of emotion sought, then wound around his consciousness, and her touch was intensified a hundredfold.

"No, don't make me hard," he whispered, a laugh in his voice. "I can do it myself."

Rolling onto his side with her still in his arms, he dipped his tongue into the small indentation at her throat. Slowly, he drifted kisses all the way down to the satin swell of her breast, his mouth leaving a cool, wet trail.

Kendra moaned aloud and he smiled.

Removing her hand from his erection, he wound her fingers around another part of him, letting her hold them. Mentally, he explained what made him feel good and she continued to stroke him just the way he loved it.

His lips lavished her nipple with attention. Such beautiful breasts, he thought. Like Kendra's, yet not like hers. Different enough to make him aware he was with someone else. He hoped it was her turn to feel new and different responses welling inside, tugging and pulling as if it were her first time.

He dipped his fingers into her, seeking to create moisture and warmth. Finding what he sought, he experienced masculine pride that it was *his* touch that caused that response. He didn't know *how* he knew she had never been this excited before, but he did. Her excitement added to his own, already intense, pleasure.

Her eyes were closed, her head drifting from side to side in the ecstasy from his lovemaking. Her hand reached out to hold him again, soft fingertips tingling against the sensitive tip of him, creating havoc with every second that sped past in lightning-slow confusion.

Overwhelming sensations he'd never experienced before flooded through him, taking his breath away with the wonder of them all. Jumbled, disconnected thoughts and feelings flooded in; all incomplete, all questions—all overwhelming.

She heard a little of his thoughts and wonderful, tinkling laughter bubbled from her throat. She wrapped her arm around him, her palm rubbing more heat enticingly against his back and side before she gave him a squeeze. *You're so very special.*

Still his thoughts were disjointed, although he tried to let her know just how terribly special she made him feel.

My God! Don't help me.... You're as wonderfully frightened as I.... So beautiful.... Laughter goes with unions.... It's so very, very...

He wasn't aware when they removed their clothing, exposing themselves to each other as naked physically as they were mentally.

Her skin was ambrosial, her touch more erotic than anything he'd ever known before.

"Is it you or me?" he asked in wonderment.

"You. Just you."

He believed her. His hands stroked her hips and inner thighs, reluctant to end the wonderful connection, but needing to unite in man's most elementary way.

Kendra moaned again. Her breath was light and airy, as shallow as his. She let her hand drift over his hand, loving the feel of his touch so much, she wanted to experience it in every way. Finally she led his hand to the small of her back and pressed herself against him.

Dan knew she was as ready for him as he was for her. Though he was confident he could still maintain some last shred of control, with the first plunge into the softness of her he was gone, riding rainbows through a thunderstorm so loud and frightening, so wicked and wonderful, that he thought he'd been struck by lightning. Brilliant and varied colors exploded in his head. Her own tightening and arching told him she was exploding, too. They were wrapped together in ecstasy, and clinging to sanity—just barely.

His breathing slowed, breath by breath, matching hers as they lay in each other's arms, coping with the unbelievable while reality lay in the quiet around them.

He brushed her hair away from her cheek. "Are you all right?"

She smiled, her eyes still closed, as she nodded.

"Did you do that?" he murmured.

Slowly, with effort, she opened her eyes and stared up at him. "I had nothing to do with it. I had no idea...."

He already knew but needed the confirmation. It was his turn to grin. "Honey, that had to be something for Kinsey to shout about. For both of us."

Her dark eyes widened. "Is that why your species is so very preoccupied with sex?"

Dan chuckled, then sought the soft skin on her neck. "Is that what you think? That humans are preoccupied with sex?"

She smiled. "We were told not to have sex with any human. It could lead to pregnancy, without first analyzing the genes for disease and faulty traits." She nuzzled her head against his chest and he loved the feel of her. "I just didn't know."

"This was called the big O, honey."

"Why would anyone purposely keep this from themselves? That felt so wonderful, surely they'd want to share it with anyone."

Dan chuckled. "It doesn't happen with just anyone. Some people *never* feel what you and I just did."

"But why? Anything that wonderful should be experienced all the time, not just once or twice."

Deep-throated laughter echoed in the darkness. "I agree. Wanna try again?"

She frowned, her mind still on the original question. "Then why us?" Her brow cleared. "I remember. Chemicals."

"Chemicals?"

She nodded. "Human chemical reaction is very strong in likes. And some women—and men—become addicted to a chemical called sebum. It's created and exchanged in kissing."

"What?" He squinted through the dappled darkness. The full moon shone through the cedar hills around them, lighting the clearing just enough for him to see her face.

"It's . . ." she began.

"I heard you, I just don't believe you. You mean that men and women are attracted because of *chemical reactions* to each other?"

She nodded. "We studied it before I came here."

"How do you make love on your planet?"

She looked surprised. "We don't. Reproduction is the main reason for sex and we have reserved that function for the laboratory. Now I wonder why we eliminated this experience." She frowned. "It mustn't be that freeing for our people. Perhaps we don't have that chemical attraction. I was never aware of it before."

He moved his hips, thrusting into her again. Surprisingly, he could make love a second time. In fact he didn't think he could get enough of her. "I don't care what you call it, this was more than a chemical reaction. Much more."

Her arms squeezed his waist, then lingered to caress the bunched muscles in his back. "I don't care what it is, either. I want more," she whispered.

His moan was his agreement. His actions followed through until they were nothing but a tangle of arms and legs and overflowing emotions.

It seemed so natural to make love to Kendra, yet so new and different an experience. Emotions he hadn't dealt with before threatened to overcome him in a mélange of feelings he wasn't able to sort through. In ways he couldn't understand, this Kendra was different from his wife, and yet he felt as if he'd made peace with his wife's ghost by making love to this Kendra.

When they both were sated, sleep overcame him. His last thought had nothing to do with his dead wife. It had everything to do with the caring woman who had cradled him in her arms while he'd cried in both joy and mourning.

DAN ANGLED THE RAFT toward the American side of the thousand-foot cliffs as they maneuvered through another section of rapids. The white-water segments weren't really difficult, just a normal degree of caution had to be observed.

He grinned at Kendra, who sat in the bow of the boat, her eyes glued to the whitecapped waves swirling rapidly below.

They had made love off and on all night, and again early this morning. He couldn't get enough of her, and when he thought he had, she wanted him again. She was as eager to come to him as he was to be with her.

Somehow, whether she was alien or not, he would do everything in his power to keep her with him.

Oh, he knew, deep down, that she wasn't Kendra. He was reminded of it each time she spoke of subjects Kendra wouldn't have been interested in, each time she tried a new way to make love—something that had always frightened the old Kendra. Each time she looked at him it was as if she was offering all her thoughts to him at one time. If he could have read the old Kendra as well as he was getting to know the new Kendra, they'd have been so much better off....

And, although she wasn't the old Kendra, he couldn't shake the feeling that he was making up to his wife, as well. Where he'd been strong and silent before, now he revealed his tenderness and vulnerability. All his regrets were being soothed and patched over by allowing the new Kendra to delve into his mistakes and his sorrow. It wasn't logical, he knew, but it helped ease his already-confused state of mind.

"This is so beautiful," she murmured, looking at the pale blue patch of sky between the tall earth-toned cliffs. Then she spotted a bird and squinted her eyes to get a better look. "The peregrine falcon," she whispered with awe in her voice.

"You don't have them?" He followed her glance to see the falcon drift playfully on the air currents.

"No, nothing so exotic. We have *barbums* and such, but that's about all that's left of the animals of our world."

"Barbums?"

She nodded absently, her gaze still fixed on the bird's flight. "They're little animals that are a cross between a lizard and a worm. They speak a language similar to a porpoise."

"My God!"

She glanced over at him, surprise written on her face. "What's wrong?"

He gave a weak smile. "They sound horrible."

"They're very useful fellows. They dig up the damp earth without disturbing new growth. They resist disease and are harmless to us. Besides, they breathe our atmosphere. They let us know through their own language when our soil and atmosphere need help."

He nodded, pretending he was too busy to pay attention to her as he steered the boat. Her eyes were focused on him, as if she was finally willing to acknowledge the difference in their...cultures. He said what was on his mind. "Here, a bar bum is someone who hangs out at a bar and leeches drinks."

It was good to hear her laughter. Different from his wife's, it began deep and moved up the scale slowly, sounding much like a delicate musical instrument.

"I forget how some of our language meshes," she said finally.

"I'm sure there are other similarities, but I'm at a loss to remember them just now," he said dryly, realizing just how little he had asked her about her world. The questions came back again, forcing their way to the forefront.

Kendra sighed. *In time, Dan. But not now. Let us just enjoy today.*

The words were clear although her mouth never moved. He was glad to shift the time of confrontation away from the here and now. Their relationship was too sweet, too new, to stress with more information yet.

He wanted to hold her in his arms and breathe in the scent of her own special perfume. He wanted her head near his heart where she could listen to the rhythm that she had created in him, feel the peace she had given him. "Would you like to go dancing tonight?" he asked abruptly.

She looked surprised. "Dancing? On the river?"

Dan looked even more shocked. "Can you dance on the river?"

"No, but . . ."

He laughed, relieved that there wasn't another talent she had that he wasn't aware of. "I meant at the trading post at Lajitas. We'll be passing there around four this afternoon. They usually have a dance once a week and I heard there's one tonight."

Her glance was filled with shy anticipation. "I'd love to. Will we be allowed in even though we are in shorts?"

She was so worldly and yet so naive. It was an intoxicating combination—one that infiltrated his defenses more than he cared to admit. "We'll worry about that when the time comes." His gruff response and his need to concentrate on boat maneuvers ended their conversation.

They hit the banks of Lajitas just after four o'clock and stored the raft, complete with supplies, in the boathouse one of the raft tours used. Then, hand in hand, they walked to the hotel, booking a room for the night. While Kendra showered, Dan stepped into the boutique and bought her a Mexican broom skirt in magenta and pink and a pink T-shirt. A pair of Mexican sandals completed the outfit.

After she opened her gifts and gave him wonderful, sweet, drugging kisses for each one, he made slow, deliberate love to her on the king-size bed. They slept for an hour and when he awoke, he was replete, never before having experienced such a sense of satisfaction. It had to be because of Kendra's brimming happiness.

The party had begun early, and on the trading-post patio a band was playing pure Mexican salsa music, loud, with a beat. The beer-drinking crowd kept time, tapping their booted toes on the uneven concrete. Others danced, circling the floor in counterclockwise steps, laughing and drinking between times.

The patio was crowded with Mexicans and Americans alike. Dan held a laughing Kendra in his arms, her face tilted up toward his as he led her around the floor. Their feet shuffled, and her legs entwined with his, heating him to a point where all he wanted was to be deep inside her warmth, rocking against her. Possessing her. Telling himself that it would come in due time, he forced himself to relax and began to enjoy the tension they both knew was building to a fever pitch.

Meanwhile they pretended they fit into the motley group on the trading-post patio. Kendra reached up, wrapping her arms around his neck, and pulled his head down to her lips. "You are a very wonderful, special man, Dan Lovejoy," she whispered.

His answer was a dizzying kiss that had her closing her eyes and wrapping her arms even tighter around his neck. Feelings he'd thought were long submerged arced through his body. He was a teenager again, with Kendra in his arms and the hope of his youthful happiness in the future. Only this time the happiness was even stronger; this Kendra was wiser and more responsible for her actions, and she was pulling him inexorably toward her with a chain of steel.

She drew back, touching his cheek with her hand. "I'm not really Kendra."

He covered her hand, pressing it to his skin as if light contact wasn't enough—not nearly enough. "You need to read my mind more often," he said, his voice rasping in a low whisper. "I know who you are. This is different. It's better."

She smiled in delight at his understanding. They danced around the room.

Dan didn't know how he would be without her for the rest of his life, but he had her now. She was his. For the moment. For the time. For the loving.

Suddenly Kendra pulled back and looked around, a quizzical frown marring her brow.

"Are you coming down with a headache, honey?"

She drew him toward her and whispered in his ear. "Pretend you're down at the river," she ordered. "See the river and concentrate on it."

Her body was stiff in his arms. He pulled her even closer. "Why?"

"Block yourself!" she whispered again, her breath a hiss against his neck.

A light probe touched his mind and he stiffened, too.

Fear of whatever she feared shot through him. He obeyed by thinking of the sound of the river. The trickle turned to a roar as he concentrated everything he had on it.

The probe came again, harder.

He continued to concentrate.

He heard a squeak and thought of a night bird finding a mouse's nest. Dinner.

A lizard squiggled on the muddy riverbank before hopping to a low mesquite branch and watching the festivities, its throat popping out into a red balloon in time with the beat of the music.

All the while, the river was the focus of his thoughts. Nothing else mattered.

The probe retreated. Still he listened to the river sounds.

The music stopped, then began again. He didn't notice, just continued to shuffle his feet automatically to whatever beat was available, or to no beat at all.

The next probe was so strong it hurt. It prodded at him so sharply he felt as if it might pierce his brain. It took all his concentration to hold his vision of the river. He imagined the gurgling sound the water made as one of the passengers on the rowboat stuck their hand in the swiftly moving current. He could hear it, see the finger in the water. The water was night-dark, swift-moving.

The probe retreated once again.

But this time, with a flash of recognition, he knew the person who had done it. A tall, lean cowboy wearing boots that looked as if they were meant for riding and not for show, stood by the low adobe-patio wall, a long-neck beer in his hand. A sweat-stained black hat pulled low kept his face in shadow. He was menacing. Then the image disappeared.

Dan kept dancing, unaware he was dragging Kendra around the circle with him.

She patted his neck. "It's okay."

Still he moved.

"You're hurting me. Stop. It's gone now."

He took another two-step.

Her hand touched his face, turning his chin down to her gaze. "It's okay, Dan. You can stop now."

His eyes focused slowly on the beautiful woman in his arms. His breath was short, his throat dry. "What happened?"

"One of us was in the crowd. He wanted some answers so we gave them."

"But why did he probe me?" The memory of pain he should have felt was still with him. His forehead broke out in cold sweat.

"He was checking." She squirmed in his grasp. "You're hurting me."

As if it were someone else's body, he looked at his hand holding hers. Her fingers were squashed together like a cluster of all-white lead pencils. With an effort, he relaxed his grip.

She gave a sigh, as her hand drifted back to his shoulder. "I'm very sorry."

"I want answers, too." His voice was curt. He didn't care. His legs were leaden weights; tension sang through every muscle in his body. "Let's find the son of a—"

"Not here. Not now."

"He's here. I saw him." Dan's gaze darted around the wall in an effort to spot the man. "I want his damn hide."

"Not now."

"Did he hurt you, too?"

She smiled. "No. He just wanted information. I gave him the answers. He's one of us, Dan, and he's here to ensure that Herfronites have guidance while they're here."

"I don't give a damn what he's supposed to do. He damn well won't hurt you and I'll make him pay for hurting me."

"He's gone."

He took a deep breath and forced his shoulders to relax. For the first time Dan noticed that while everyone was dancing to a fast tune, he was still moving to a ballad. Quickly he grabbed her hand and led her off the patio and into the darkness toward the river.

As he passed one of the picnic tables where he had left their drinks, he picked up two cans of Coors beer from an open six-pack.

"What did you take?" she asked.

"Silver bullets," Dan answered, referring to the ad campaign the beer company had used for years. "It'll ward off werewolves."

When they reached the bank he realized the river sounds were exactly as he'd imagined them earlier. Had he actually heard them or had he made them up from his own recollections?

"You heard them," she replied.

"How do you know?"

"I was the first probe."

He remembered the first one, so soft and gentle compared to the others. "Why?"

"To make sure you were doing what I told you to do."

"And what would you have done if I hadn't?"

She shrugged, and the moonlight filtered through her hair as it moved. "I don't know. I might have tried to cocoon your mind myself, but then they would know I was protecting you."

"From what?"

"Our probe."

"Ours? Yours and his?"

"No, 'ours' as in 'our race,'" she explained. "We are a collective society. Everything we do is for the benefit of all of us. Not just 'I' or 'me.'"

"You're three-quarters human and you live in a collective society?" he accused.

"Right," she confirmed.

"Then why protect me?"

She searched his gaze, her forehead marred by wrinkles as she tried to reason out her own behavior. "I don't know. I didn't want them to know how much we care for each other. It's against the rules to get involved with humans. If we do, we can get so lost in your world we may not want to return to our own. The Elders have explained it to us, but it is still beyond our wisdom."

One idea came through clearly, though. She cared for him. If he could persuade her to stay, he'd have another chance at happiness.

"Stay with me. Don't go back."

She shook her head, and in the moonlight her hair looked like silver. "It wouldn't work. They'd find us."

"How many miles can a probe reach?"

"If they're trying hard, maybe a mile or two."

"Kind of like a citizens-band radio? That can be overcome." His thoughts were whirling.

"It's not that easy to hide."

"Not if they can't find you to probe your mind."

"They can search you out, too," she reminded him gently.

"How? I'm one of the millions who live here. You're the one they can spot."

She shook her head. "Once a mind is probed, we can find you easily, as if there was a chemical trace."

He smiled ferally. "But they didn't probe my mind. They just attempted to."

Fleeting hope eased the strain in her face. "Do you think so?"

Dan chuckled. Finally, something was falling under his control. "Yes, I think so. We'll figure it out. I promise."

Her smile slowly melted. "It doesn't matter. I've broken too many rules already. I must go back. I must do my job and make amends. Too many Herfronites are counting on me," she whispered, as if afraid to be overheard. "But at least for a little while longer, I want to pretend we don't have to leave each other." She stared down at the rocky ground, her demeanor suddenly shy. "I want to be with you."

Dan felt his heartbeat quicken. He'd fight for her forever if he could. "At least we agree on something," he said with a sigh. "Don't worry. We'll work it out." He said it far more confidently than he felt.

Kendra leaned her head against his chest and he inhaled the scent of her hair. Crickets sang, water lapped against the shoreline, stars twinkled above. Despite the idyllic situation, the depth of his emotions for the woman in his arms and the thought of parting from her pained him. Placing his thumb under her chin, Dan lifted her face to the moonlight. He stared at her, seeing every feature accented in the silver glow.

How could a race of people be so sophisticated in some ways while so naive in others? He didn't understand. He *couldn't* understand. A small voice in the back of his mind told him he was playing with fire, thinking he could kidnap her from what she considered her own people. But he ignored it. He wanted her; she wanted him. That was all that mattered. All other warnings were useless.

"Don't get me confused any more than I already am," she whispered. Apparently she was reading his thoughts again.

"As long as you know that confusion isn't my problem, too, honey. I'm not confused. I'm determined."

"This won't last forever. I must go home."

"Just a few extra days together," he told her.

"A few extra days," she repeated softly, her full mouth turning up in a sad smile.

His lips brushed hers, his heart expanding with all the loving emotions she brought out in him. "Let's get out of here," he said, releasing his grip on her waist and reaching for her hand. Together, they walked up the tree-shadowed path toward the hotel.

5

As dawn broke over the high desert, Dan and Kendra pushed the raft away from the riverbank. Minutes later, the trading post was out of sight.

The farther away from Lajitas they got, the more Dan relaxed. In contrast, the farther away they got, the more tense Kendra became. When he saw the whites of her knuckles on the raft rope, he demanded, "What is it?"

"Nothing."

"Don't tell me that. Talk to me." His voice dropped. "I need to know, honey."

Her eyes widened at his endearment. She stared up at him, then gently probed his thoughts. He opened completely, letting her feel the rush of love that filled his very being.

"But for which Kendra?" she asked softly. Her wide eyes stared at him as if unable to see—or read—the answer.

"This Kendra. You."

She shook her head as if to ease the confusion. "I don't know. I don't think you really know how to separate us."

"I thought you could read my mind."

"I can't read your emotions, Dan. And I feel confused. I'm not sure your feelings are for me." Her breathing was shallow. He'd swear she was frightened. "I have never felt this way and it is not a good feeling."

"You're feeling the same doubt and anxiety all of us humans experience."

She digested his words, ignoring the sarcasm just below the surface. Then she pushed her hair back absently, her mind still on the emotions consuming her. "How do you know that's what it is?"

"Because I love you." He stopped paddling for a moment and tried to think of the words he needed. "I think you are what I was looking for when I fell in love with the other Kendra. With you, I just *know*."

His words didn't ease her state of mind. If anything, she looked a little more frightened. "I need to know for sure that this is the name of what I'm feeling."

"No, you don't. At least not right this minute. Take your time." He grinned, softening his words. "We have another two days."

Kendra's brows drew together. "We're less than a day away from the spaceship. When we reach the place, you will have to continue on without me."

"Without you?"

It was Kendra's turn to smile, even though it wasn't a happy look. "I must go home and you must continue your own personal journey. We don't have a choice."

An overwhelming sadness encompassed him but he reined it in and pretended she hadn't said that. There was no use arguing with her right now. She wouldn't hear him. But later, when he held her in his arms and made love to her, he would persuade her to stay. Dan used his paddle as a rudder over a stretch of minor rapids. "What about my memories? Will you take those recollections of our time together away from me?"

"Don't ask me yet," she implored. Her eyes closed as if she could keep the need to make those decisions at bay by denying them. "I don't know what to do."

He kept his silence after that. After the mind probe last night from a source completely foreign to him, he had an idea just how powerful her race was. And how impotent he felt. Impotent! Hell, he was living in a nightmare! He was not only in fear of losing the woman he'd just found and now loved, he was also in fear of being probed—an experience that was like a rape of the mind.

"I know it seems that way," Kendra said, and he realized she'd been able to read his thoughts without giving even the gentlest probe that time. She was as good as any pickpocket on the streets of Dickens's London.

"It *is* that way," he stated emphatically. "I don't seem to have any control over others' thoughts or actions, let alone my own."

"Don't be bitter," she admonished softly.

But his lazy mood had vanished, and was replaced by tension that was great enough for both of them. "Then don't tell me what to do."

Dan kept the raft slightly to the right of the center of the river. In tense silence, they traveled downstream, both caught up in their own tangled reflections.

If he thought that losing Kendra had been hell, he was wrong. Hell on earth was losing Kendra twice.

The most frustrating thing of all was that he had no control over either loss. He couldn't play white knight and charge in to rescue her. He couldn't protect her from Earth's evils—or unearthly evils, either, for that matter.

Hell, he didn't even know which Kendra he was feeling confused about! Contrary to what he'd said, both women, although so very different from each other, were blending together in his mind. They were becoming one—a woman who was neither one nor the other but a combination of both, plus some indescribable, intangible something else.

Kendra leaned forward, touching his arm. "Please. Don't worry now. There will be time enough later."

"What do you care?" he retorted, surprised at his own bitterness showing so readily. "You'll be gone soon and I'll still be here. Without you." He paddled the raft over to the Mexican side and secured it to a small tree overhanging the water.

"Before I leave, I promise I'll help you feel better." Her soothing voice made him even angrier.

"Dammit!" he yelled, turning around to face her, his hands itching to close around her shoulders and shake some sense into her. "Can't you read my mind enough to know that that's the *last* thing I want you to do? This is *my* misery! *My* heartache. *My* damn pain! Don't take it away from me!"

His hands clamped on her small shoulders, but instead of shaking her, they soothed through the T-shirt material to the soft skin below. He took a deep shuddering breath, then spoke in a low voice. "I need to get *through* this, not ignore it."

Her gaze was so tender he wanted to cry. "I try, Dan, but I don't understand the human logic behind that thought. If you can be helped so you will not feel so badly, why not take advantage of it?"

His grin tight, he realized he regretted his outburst; she really didn't understand. "I guess it's just the wild and crazy human in me."

Kendra reached up and, with gentle fingers, soothed his taut jawline. It was the only thing she could give him, and she needed to help. He was her love and she was sure there would be no other to take his place. If anyone had fewer choices than Dan, it was her. But she couldn't speak of that just now; her hands would simply have to translate the message of just how special he was to her.

It helped ease a little of his tension when he forced his muscles to go limp, stopped resisting her help. Her unspoken feelings translated into the tender yet sensual touch of her soothing fingers. He needed her touch.

He needed her.

He took another breath and forced himself to calm down. She shouldn't leave him. "Kendra," he began, but her fingers drifted across his lips to silence the words she knew he would say.

"We both know I don't belong here, Dan. I need to be with my people. I know the rules there—I can live with what is expected and what is not considered correct. Herfronite laws are basic and logical, and that makes it much easier to live in my society than in yours. My people have been good and kind and loving to me. I cannot repay them by desertion. It is my duty to return and share my knowledge."

Dan closed his eyes and concentrated on nothing but her touch on his skin, her birdlike bones beneath his palms, the wonderful, indescribable scent of her. Carefully he pulled her to him, resting his head on her dark hair. She fit so perfectly against him, her softness a complement to his hard body.

A falcon called to its mate as it circled aloft. The rapids behind and in front of them whispered enticingly for Dan to continue his journey. Bright sun stood overhead, daring them to remain dressed in the dizzying heat of the day.

He continued to hold her in the steel grip of his arms, loving the feel of her against him and hoping to burn the memory of this moment into his brain so that no matter what happened, he could relive this time.

"Dan," she murmured against his chest.

He felt his muscles tighten in anticipation. Was she being mind-probed again? Was Cowboy on their trail? Despite her thoughts on the matter, he knew the man would follow to ensure that she did what was expected of her. That was his damn job. He was supposed to keep Kendra from Dan. He felt the adrenaline flow at the thought. He wanted to blame someone, smash someone, hurt someone, hit someone. He wanted to . . .

"Dan, please," Kendra whispered, her breath on his flesh even warmer than the heat of the day.

"It's all right, honey. I'm here."

"I know." Her voice was muffled against his chest. "I can't breathe."

"Sorry," he said, his voice suddenly unable to project past his throat. "I keep forgetting just how fragile you are."

Kendra looked up and took a deep breath, smiling slowly. "It's all right now."

Without another word, Dan unwrapped the rope from the tree and picked up the oar. Within seconds they were back in the mainstream, safe and busy enough that he didn't have to rehash their last conversation.

They drifted with the Rio Grande current for the next two hours. Lunchtime had passed a few hours earlier, but Dan had ignored it. However, when his stomach finally protested in hunger, he brought the raft to the bank, tying up at a flat, rocky place. If the river rose any more, this shelf would probably be underwater all the way to the wall of trees farther back.

He'd thought to go through the ice chest and put together something quick for lunch. But Kendra beat him to it by jumping to the bank with a sleeping bag and the small cooler in her hand. Heart beating a special rhythm only for her, Dan watched as she walked to the far trees and spread the unzipped sleeping bag in the shade. Then she sat, cross-legged, on the downfilled material and looked at him expectantly.

Grabbing the larger ice chest, he walked to the shade she'd found, set the cooler down, then squatted next to her. "Make whatever sandwiches you want," he said abruptly.

She stared up at him, a quizzical look on her face. "Did I do something to displease you?"

"No."

"Do you hurt?"

"Yes."

"Can I help?"

"No. You won't be around to help later, so I might as well get used to the pain now." He knew he sounded childish, but he couldn't help it. In fact, he felt childish about everything to do with her. Damn! He was confused and hated the feeling of being out of control of his own life.

In silence Kendra efficiently spread sandwich fixings over the top of the ice chest. "Are you reading my mind?"

She began putting together a sandwich. Her head bobbed up and down.

"Why aren't I feeling it?" he asked, wondering if she was probing or reading his body language. If she was feeling him out—or *malking*—shouldn't he know it?

"You're too busy being angry."

"Are you telling me I'm not paying attention?"

Again, Kendra nodded. "If someone is gentle enough and the other person is preoccupied, it could be done without noticing the intrusion."

Dan filed that information away. If he was going to win this war of nerves, he'd better learn how to fight.

He inhaled his sandwich, then leaned back, crossed his arms behind his head and stared up at the pale blue sky. "Teach me how to read minds."

Kendra took the last dainty bite of her sandwich. "That takes much practice, and I won't be here long enough to do that."

"How far away is your spaceship?"

She thought hard for a moment. "Closer than we thought. I saw the crest of the mountain as we took the last turn. About two hours from here."

"Then try to teach me in the next two hours."

Kendra sighed, carefully placing her paper plate in the bag they'd been using for trash. "Do you meditate?"

"I've never tried before."

"Lie back, hands at your sides, legs straight."

He stared over at her. "I thought I was supposed to sit cross-legged and put my hands in a praying position."

"Not unless you're used to praying in that position," she answered dryly. "I've never seen you sit that way. It wouldn't make sense to start now, because in five minutes you'd be very uncomfortable and unable to concentrate."

Dan hated it when she was more logical than he was. Grudgingly, he complied. Staring at her, he silently demanded the next instruction.

She smiled sweetly and his anger dissipated. Then he realized she'd read his thoughts again. "You weren't supposed to know that."

Her smile widened. "That's what made it all the sweeter."

Don't get too smug, he malked. *You may not be able to do it after this.*

"Lie still," she said aloud, obviously unwilling to let him know whether or not she received that message. "Now, close your eyes."

He did as he was told. Her tone dropped even lower, becoming more dulcet. "Begin by focusing on the sounds of the wind, the river, the bird's cries."

He tried, but thoughts kept flooding him. They still had to repack the raft, then go through the next two sets of rapids....

"Push all those thoughts away, very gently, very slowly, so you won't interrupt your own decelerating pulse rate."

Her voice was gentle, sunshine warm and mesmerizing, and he felt himself relaxing even more. "Try doing what you did last night when I told you about the probe, only this time you'll go deeper."

He continued to concentrate on everything around him while keeping himself distant from it all.

"Give all your weight to the ground, Dan. Let it absorb you so you are one with the warmth of this Earth."

Thoughts continued to bombard him, but he ignored them altogether by concentrating on the natural sounds around him.

"Breathe from the diaphragm, fill the center of your heart with the steady heat of life, then allow it to radiate through the rest of you."

Dan tried to follow her directions as best he could. Despite his gentle nudging-away of those thoughts that came at him like darts, he began to feel as if he were floating slightly above the ground. His chest felt the warmth of the sun and it seemed to seep into every muscle and vein.

"Now, pretend you can reach out to me as if we had a cord connecting the two of us."

Dan imagined what she was saying, reaching toward Kendra only to find she was already there, wrapping him in her arms and holding him securely. It wasn't until he looked down that he realized he was flying across the face of the Earth.

You're doing well, Dan, he felt Kendra say.

Don't distract me, he thought back.

Her answer was a chuckle. It was a wonderful, emotional sound that vibrated into the very center of him.

Dan opened his eyes and Earth rushed back with a snap. "Did you talk to me?"

Kendra nodded, her face a wreath of a smile.

"Did I do it or did you draw it from me?"

"You did it."

He sat up, a grin pulling at his mouth and a glint in his blue eyes. "I really did?"

"Yes, but you have a long way to go, Dan. This was just an experiment to prove you have the capability. I'm willing to be read and therefore am an easy channel for connection. Most of your kind are not that way. You have a lot more practice to do."

He still wanted confirmation. "But I *did* do it, didn't I?"

"You did."

"Teach me more," he demanded.

"Not now." Her smile waned and her gaze darted toward the river. "We have to go."

Dan followed her gaze but saw nothing. "Is he here?"

"I think so." She looked at the remains of their picnic and pretended she needed to clean up. "I thought I felt him earlier."

"Then he *is* following?"

"I think so," Kendra finally acknowledged, twirling the trash sack and tying it with a twist tie. "Let's get going."

"Are you afraid?"

"A little. He was very angry last night when he knew I might have broken a few rules."

Dan raised a brow. "*Might* have?"

"All right. *Did*," she corrected. "But I don't want to talk about it."

Dan stood, too keyed up to sit. He began pacing. "I don't care about the bastard, but if he wants to harm you in any way, he'll have to deal with me, first."

"This is not your problem, Dan."

"But—"

"No buts. Promise me."

"I won't." He sat back down, his face a grim mask. "If I see the bas—"

"No more." She held up her hand to stop his words. "He is a Guardian. He has the authority to check on me. He will not hurt me."

It wouldn't do any good arguing with her. Her mind was made up.

It took five minutes to reload and shove off. And, for Dan, each of those minutes was charged with reluctance. Every wave they took, every turn of the oar, brought him closer to his separation from Kendra. They wouldn't have one more night together, after all. Today was the day they would part, and he would be alone again—without either of the two women he had loved.

He knew the feelings he had for this Kendra were love, but he didn't want to feel this way. *Love* was the name for something that he didn't want to feel, hear about or experience again. It was too painful. Besides, the emotions he felt for this Kendra and his wife mixed so completely together, that sometimes he couldn't tell the two women apart. They were entwined like several strands of a thread—so tightly that they couldn't be separated into single filaments. Perhaps in time it might change, but right now he was so connected to this woman, he couldn't remember her differences from the other. He was sure he knew the distinction; he just chose not to think about it.

And now he was losing both women. It didn't matter why; either way, he was going to hurt. Unless he could put the necessary words together to convince her to stay with him.

"Pull up here." She motioned toward a shallow harbor in the next bend in the river.

Dan did as he was told, paddling over to the American side of the river. Ducking under several willow trees, he anchored to one. After Kendra jumped ashore, Dan followed, then pulled the raft up on the dry, slab-stone bank, shielding it from prying river eyes.

A rat scurried through the underbrush, but Kendra ignored it as she stared up at the face of the mountain. All her attention was focused on the jagged rocks above them. Dan couldn't see a thing. Like all the other high cliffs, it was pitted with holes and shallow caves; nothing appeared different.

Then she brought her attention back to Dan, and her luminous eyes stared at him with as much sadness as he felt in his own heart. "I will miss you, Dan Lovejoy," she stated softly. "I will miss you so very much."

"Stay," he whispered around the tears caught in his throat. He'd promised himself he wouldn't beg, but he did. "Stay with me."

"I can't. I have broken so many rules already, I must do this. Please leave, now," she said.

Dan felt defeat like he'd never felt it before. "Are you sure?"

"Yes."

But he couldn't let go that easily. "I'll wait here for a little while, just in case you change your mind. If you don't come back down in the next ten minutes, then I'll leave."

"Dan," she began.

He kissed her lips. "Shh. I'm going to wait for ten minutes, that's all. If I didn't, I would never know that I'd given you one last chance to change your mind, and I would always wonder. This way, I'll know you chose it."

She hesitated, then nodded. "All right. But I will not return."

She tilted her head and placed a kiss in the palm of his hand. Tears sheened her gaze as she stared up at him. Cradling it against her cheek, she silently implored him to let her go.

Dan had no choice. His hands reluctantly dropped to his sides. "Goodbye, Kendra Lovejoy. I'll never forget you."

"You will never speak of me to anyone?"

He shook his head. A small sad smile tugged at his full mouth. "No. Besides, who would believe?"

"Who would believe?" she repeated softly. "Goodbye." With a gentle touch on his cheek, she turned and began the climb up the slope. Her footing was sure and secure as she twisted and turned on a path he would have sworn wasn't there.

She sidled sideways in spots and Dan thought that she would fall. *Stop it!* he told himself. This was her territory, not his. He wasn't a white knight or a heroic savior of some kind. In fact, she was the one in charge, not the other way around.

When he lost sight of her, a sense of panic tore at his chest. He knew what he'd promised, he knew she didn't want him with her anymore. Just the same, he couldn't remain here and not know that she was safe. Instead, he started to follow close behind. She was too preoccupied with her quest to realize he was in back of her, and she continued on her chosen path. They were heading for a shallow shelf about three-quarters up the side of the mountain. He looked down once and realized that the only way to see the path would have been from the top; the shrubs at the bottom made it invisible.

When she stopped and faced a shallow opening, he wasn't far behind her. He halted, holding his breath as he watched her turn into the opening. He hoped she couldn't hear his heavy breathing. When she'd disappeared, he climbed the rest of the way to reach the narrowest part of the ledge.

The sight in front of him made his breath quicken even more, then threatened to clog his throat. Nestled in the shallow dirt hollow, like a newborn baby cuddled in its mother's arms, was a cigar-shaped ship. It was the size of a small blimp or submarine, without visible rudder, deck, wings or windows.

"Holy hell," he muttered under his breath. He was paralyzed by the fact that the object in front of him was real. But so was everything—*everything* that had happened to him in the past three days.

Kendra had walked past the rear and along the broad side until she reached the front. The outer skin of the capsule wasn't bright and shiny or metallic as he'd expected. It was a dull blue-gray color with a slightly dimpled texture that didn't reflect light. Dan reached out and felt the podlike ship. Even though it was in a cool place and the sun wasn't shining on it, the outside, calluslike skin was warm to the touch.

Kendra stood in front of the conelike capsule, gazing upward as she placed her hands, palms up, on the underskin. After a few seconds, a whine—more like a wind sigh—began, strengthening in volume the longer it went on.

Dan wanted to leave. Hell, he wanted to disappear! Every instinct for survival told him to get out of there and run for his life. But he couldn't move.

He saw Kendra go to the front side closest to the stone wall, so he followed a short distance behind. He was amazed to see that the whining sound, which had now stopped, must have been the ramp he now saw folded out from the ship. He watched as Kendra stepped on a circular black disk at the base, and it lifted, taking her to the entrance. She disappeared and Dan waited for something to happen. Nothing did. But the disk reappeared, and he stepped on it, hoping to hell there were no more surprises inside. He didn't want to fight a Herfronite or see Cowboy anytime soon. He just wanted to make sure that Kendra was all right.

When Dan walked inside, a cool moistness envel-
oped him. It was similar to the feeling of a green-
house; damp, cool air filled with the scents of earth
and growing things. He looked around but there were
no plants, no soil, no air-conditioning ducts that he
could see. Instead, with the exception of the one wall
of buttons, lights and screens, it looked like the bare
lobby of any navy ship.

With her back to him, Kendra dropped her hand
from a spot next to the far door, waited for a panel to
open, then stepped over the threshold into what
looked like a laboratory.

At least, he thought it was a laboratory. It didn't
have the usual trays and utensils he was familiar with,
but it did hold a few large pieces of equipment that resembled body scanners or New Age X-ray machines.

Kendra stood in front of one such machine that resembled a freestanding shower. She emitted a series
of strange mouselike sounds. It must have been another identifying device, for the whirring began again;
then a large panel opened to expose the lab instru-
ments he'd expected to see earlier.

After she'd punched a few buttons on a side panel,
the large glass "shower" door opened and she quickly
stripped off her clothing, then stepped inside. The
door closed and Kendra stood still, her arms at her
sides, her body straight. Her head tilted toward the
top corner of the cubicle, where numbers and sym-
bols began to spew across a screen.

Dan couldn't move, couldn't yell, couldn't do anything but watch in fascination as Kendra was scanned—naked, head to toe—by a giant camera and three free-moving pads that touched her body in key spots. It was over in two or three minutes. The noise stopped, leaving the normal, dull sounds of the ship to fill the space. The door snapped open and she stepped out, her expression quizzical and wondrous at the same time.

He stepped forward. "Kendra."

She froze, then slowly turned around and faced him, her head tilted in that disarming way she had. The look in her eyes was as surprised and shocked as he felt. "You shouldn't be here."

"I needed to be sure you made it safely," he said simply.

She seemed distracted. "Did anyone follow you?"

"No one's out there," he assured her. Before she could protest, he wrapped his arms around her slim form. She wasn't cold, but her stiffness surprised him. "Tell me what's wrong. You look like somebody socked you in the stomach."

"Try to read me," she replied, finally reaching up and wrapping her arms around him.

He tried but images blended together, not making any sense. "I can't," he finally said.

She must have understood why. She looked disbelieving and yet like she'd seen a miracle. "I'm carrying a child."

Heat swept through him and he felt an overwhelming protectiveness. "It's my child, too."

"Of course. You're the only man I've been with." She smiled.

He placed a gentle kiss on her slightly parted lips, then held her close to him, hoping she could read his jumbled emotions and know how wonderful the news was. "We have to leave."

"Leave?" she repeated slowly. "I can't. I must go back to my people. I have so much to learn. And so much to teach. Oh, Dan." She grinned as if the sun was in her smile. "Isn't it wonderful? We made a child! I never thought I would be able to fulfill that role. At my home, I wasn't chosen for that field, but now I'm going to do it!"

She obviously didn't understand the problem. Dan would explain it as calmly as he could. "You can't go back now. That's *my* child you're carrying!"

"You helped, but it's really my child now." She touched his cheek to help fend off some of his anger. "I will take good care of her. I promise."

Her words finally got through the mass of emotions spilling everywhere. "A girl? You already know it's a girl?"

She nodded, her smile so large it warmed everything in the room—everything except his heart. "A girl. She'll be so pretty, Dan. I'm sure our genes are good. But we don't have any choice, do we? The genes were produced at random, by our bodies, instead of being selected correctly, in a laboratory."

"I want her, Kendra." He spoke slowly and distinctly, as if his message wasn't being heard correctly. "This child is mine and she belongs here on Earth, not with your people."

"She is Herfronite, and she will remain with me," Kendra argued. "I am the mother, and have the right. We will adopt a father to share the responsibility of raising the child until she goes to learning."

"You don't have to adopt a father," he retorted angrily. "I'm already here. I'll be part of her raising. The child is mine. She will learn about being a human. After all, she'll be even more human than you are."

Kendra pulled out of his arms and reached for her clothes, slipping them on quickly to hide her beautiful body from his possessive eyes. When she was through, she faced him with straightforward dignity and a firmness that told him just how stubborn she was. "There is no argument here. Since she is a part of me, the baby must remain with me. End of the discussion."

"Stay." He had to get through to her. Her stubbornness couldn't be as strong as his need to keep her with him. "Stay. Don't take my child back to your planet. What if she's an outcast? What if she . . ." He swallowed. A child.

Kendra's gaze darted to the door of the ship, then back again. "Go . . . now, Dan. Before another comes

here. Once someone sees you, I will be forced to erase
your memory."

"Kendra . . ." he began.

"No. Don't you see? I don't have a choice. I have to
stay here. It's my job. What I was trained for. I need
to complete my mission. And you need to return to
your life and begin again." It sounded more like an
order than a consolation. As if to prove her point, she
turned her back to him.

Then, reaching into her oversize bag, Kendra pulled
out a small box, took it to the counter and opened it
up to display several slides filed inside. She went directly to work, pulling them out and sliding them into
a slot on the console. Dan stood near the center of the
room, unsure what to do but knowing he wasn't leaving without a fight. She was the woman he loved, and
the child she was carrying was his. What choice did
he have? If he left, he would never see her again. Even
if she wanted to return to him, Herfronites like Cowboy would stop her. Of that much he was positive.

One by one, each of Kendra's slides was analyzed
and readings were sent to a screen in a code that Dan
could only guess at. To him, it looked like a breakdown of the slide's chemistry. But just in case, he
wanted to know for certain.

Dan went to her side and watched the screen
closely. "What's that?"

Kendra was studying the results, occasionally flip-
ping switches back and forth.

"Go away, Dan."

"Tell me."

She shrugged her shoulders as if what she was doing didn't matter. "DNA."

He was still reacting to the news that he would be a father, and it took a moment for her words to connect. When they did, Dan froze. "Whose DNA? Human?"

"Of course. I'm checking to ensure that I processed it correctly and the bulk of it is still usable." She flipped another switch.

He felt anger grow in the pit of his stomach. It was bad enough that she wanted to leave with his child, but to steal *other* human genetic material was too much to bear. "You damn well better be kidding."

She looked up, surprised at his tone. "Why would I joke about my work?"

"Your work?"

"Of course. This is the reason I was sent here."

He didn't want to know, but he had to. Whatever was happening had to be stopped. "Is this to make more Herfronites?"

"Yes. Or at least to take some of the more desirable traits and blend them with ours." She made some adjustments in her calculations.

"Destroy it," he ordered. "You have no right to take DNA from us without our permission. It's wrong."

"It's too late." She spoke calmly, continuing her work without looking at him.

"Destroy it. Now." His voice growled out the last word. His hands at his sides clenched into fists.

She didn't answer. Instead, she flipped a switch and a slide popped out.

Dan's hands reached for her shoulders again, but this time it wasn't because he was worried for her safety or concerned about her health. He was angry. "Dammit! Listen to me! You have to destroy it!"

Kendra's body went stiff. "Don't touch me." Her tone was so low and cold that he felt the icy chill of it through his anger. He didn't need to see her face.

"Give it back," Dan stated doggedly. But he forced himself to release his grip on her.

Kendra slowly faced him, her expression deceptively bland. But the words that formed in his mind were definitely hers: *Don't ever hold me in anger again.*

He glared back, thinking his own answer. *Or what?*

"Or you will not be allowed to remain conscious." She spoke the words aloud, and they echoed through the chamber like a giant rumble of thunder.

His palms still burned with the message. So many emotions flooded his system, he felt as if he was on overload.

Kendra gave a deep sigh. "Look, boyo," she began in a placating voice.

"Don't patronize me! I want what belongs to my race and I am the *only* one here who has the right to it!"

Kendra cocked her head and stared at him. "I don't understand, Dan. Men spill their seed from the time they are capable of manufacturing it. You don't seem to care where it goes or how it is destroyed. But, I didn't take semen. I took minute plugs of skin. My job is to make my people stronger so they can work more efficiently. This DNA might make that possible. It didn't hurt anyone I took it from. Why would you mind that I took it?"

"You didn't get permission."

She shook her head. "They never knew what I was doing."

"It's ours," he insisted, unable to think of anything else to say, but determined to continue his quest.

She looked at him in disgust. He'd seen that look before. He knew she was right, but he refused to give in. It was a soapbox—his soapbox—and one that he'd stand on forever. He reached over and flipped the toggle switch that spewed out the slides. She reached out to stop him but her actions were too slow. All the other slides spewed out.

"Damn you!" she cried, for the first time losing control of her anger. "You had no right to do that. You ruined them! That was a lifetime's work I cannot get back, Dan."

"Don't you get it? It wasn't yours! If you held a gun to a man's head and robbed him in a dark alley, you couldn't have stolen more! It's bad enough you want to take my child from me, but you can't steal clones of those men, too!"

Kendra stared at him as if he'd just uttered something insane.

A rage brought about by frustration filled him like fiery lava from a volcano. When it reached his brain, he couldn't move. For just a fleeting moment, he felt as if he was about to implode.

He wanted to envelop her in his arms and make her listen to the messages his heart was delivering when his tongue couldn't find the words.

Instead, he felt her soothing mental touch, cooling the anger, stroking the giant rage in him until it was manageable once more. Tangled threads of feeling wove through him, disengaging, untangling the knots. *I'm not sure I understand, but I respect your desire,* she "told" him.

Suddenly, her soothing stopped. Dan waited a moment, wondering what was different. Then he knew. Someone else was probing. He immediately blocked his thoughts by imaging a picture of the outside of the spaceship.

Kendra's gaze widened in fear. She touched his hand. "You must leave," she whispered. With urgent steps, she strode out of the room toward the exit. Her anxiety was almost as palpable as his anger had been earlier.

He followed her out, still holding the image of the exterior of the ship. The pain became more intense as the probe plumbed his thoughts. Dan knew it was Cowboy—and this time, he was allowing Dan to receive a message, as well. It was clear, concise and to the point.

The message told him to get the hell out and run. Dan realized that the slides, Kendra's pregnancy—nothing would matter if he didn't take matters in hand and leave now to fight another day. It didn't even matter that Kendra had chosen to allow him his memories. If Cowboy had his way, Dan wouldn't even be alive.

6

KENDRA LED DAN down the ramp to the rocky ground. Concentrating on speed and stealth, she maneuvered them around the side to the back of the ship. There, she stood perfectly still, trying to find Cowboy's location and probe his mind.

Cowboy probed Dan again and the pain was severe. It seemed the jerk was in love with dishing out pain. Dan closed his eyes and tried not to moan aloud. When it stopped, he took a gulp of air and prepared for the next onslaught.

It began again.

"Go with it," Kendra whispered, squeezing his hand in encouragement. "Think of nothing else but your pain, and he will feel it too."

He held his breath and concentrated on the intense sting of the needlelike probe into his thoughts. The probing seemed to hesitate, then begin again. When it withdrew, it left him weak and shaking from head to foot.

"Easy." Her other hand touched his arm as if soothing a young child. "He's close by," she whispered softly. "That's why it's so strong. You need to get out of here. You'll be safe once you clear the ship area."

"Why? He can track me anywhere. You said so yourself."

"He won't. He's after me because he knows I've broken the rules and doesn't want me to break any more. He wants to make sure that I stay here and am ready for the flight home."

Kendra quickly led him away from the ship to the top of the trail. They descended the footpath more carefully than they managed to climb it. There were no grips, no handholds, just a dizzying, straight-down track on rock, loose shale and the occasional prickly scrub. After the last probe, Dan still felt a little light-headed. It took all his concentration to focus on Kendra's back.

All he had to do was get to the boat. . . .

Just as Dan reached the shoreline, the mind probe came unexpectedly and he had to stop and hold his head to ease the pounding. As it slackened, he fumbled with the rope until it unraveled from the bush where it was tied. Scrambling into the center of the raft, he halted for a moment and stared at Kendra. He didn't want to leave her behind to fend off that jackass by herself. It wasn't fair. She should be with him.

But he didn't bother to ask her again. She knew how he felt and he knew she wouldn't change her mind. He could rant and rave, but she didn't have to do a damn thing he said. She could take his daughter and leave, and it was out of his hands. She knew what he was thinking and had answered him. Nothing more could be said. "Will you be all right?" he finally asked.

Her face was pale, her eyes dark and luminous while she took in his features as if memorizing them. Instead of speaking, she slowly nodded. But the shocked look on her face said the direct opposite. He had a feeling she knew something he wasn't telling her.

"Is it Cowboy?"

She nodded again.

"Tell him to go to hell," he growled.

"He knows about the slides." She sounded as if she was going to cry.

The feeling of satisfaction at having ruined the DNA samples stuck with him. He didn't care if Cowboy was angry. No one had the right to do what they were doing. Kendra must have heard his thoughts, for she gave him another hug.

All thoughts of revenge or anger fled with her in his arms. He couldn't make himself get into the raft alone. Despite the pain he knew would be forthcoming if he stayed, he couldn't *not* see her again. He asked the question, already knowing her answer. "Come with me," he finally managed. "Please."

Pulling back, she shook her head, her own eyes glazing with tears. "I must return. I have no choice. Herfron is my home, just as Earth is yours. Besides, I have to explain myself to my superiors. I must make my homecoming."

"Why?" He gave a crooked grin and reached for her hand. "You're three-quarters human and one-quarter Herfronite. It seems to me that you should spend at least a year or two visiting relatives. Don't you think our daughter should know this side of her family first?" It was a weak attempt at humor.

"Oh, Dan," she whispered, her emotions apparently as strained and drawn as his. "I wish..." She gave his hand a squeeze in place of the words that would not be voiced aloud.

Dan felt the probe again, but this time it was less intense. He felt the tendrils of thought wind around him, and pretended that he was on the path above. Then, suddenly, a thought radioed directly to him from their predator. One single, but very strong, decision had been made by the Herfronite who was following them. The message was clear: Cowboy was going to kill them both.

Kendra's expression told him she'd gotten the same message and was stunned. If possible, her face turned even more white. Fear sheened her eyes. Her mouth formed a small O and her gaze darted around the brush as if searching for a hiding spot.

Dan dropped her hand and reached for the oar. Finally, he was in control and knew what to do. Whether Kendra liked it or not, she was going with him. "Get in."

"Dan, I..." She looked around again.

"There's no more time. Get in!" he barked. Both of them were surprised when she did as she was told.

Pushing off from the bank, Dan headed for the center of the river where the current was swiftest. It was time to get away as fast as possible. All his attention focused on the eddies and river currents. As long as Kendra was directly behind him, he didn't need to worry about what her insane compatriot was going to do to her. He only had to make sure there was as much distance as possible between them and the maniac pursuing them. He wanted to keep them alive.

Once more he remembered Cowboy's horrible threat. A shiver zinged down his spine and he felt the icy fingers of fear invade every part of him. Even his overwhelming anger took a back seat to the thought that someone could take Kendra away for good. And she was carrying their child—a part of him.

It's okay, Kendra *malked* to him. Her hand lightly brushed his shoulder, then soothed down his back. *Really. We'll work it out. Somehow.*

Dan clenched the paddle, his knuckles turning white. "My God, Kendra. He wants to kill us *both!* It doesn't sound like this jackass wants to work anything out!"

She was silent. But her hands spoke; they continued to soothe and stroke him. With every twist and turn they took, every rapid they rode, every boulder they circumvented, Dan breathed a sigh of relief. It meant one more obstacle between them and Cowboy.

Normally, they would have rafted downriver until dusk, but with Cowboy after them, Dan felt he needed to do something different to throw him off the trail. He just wasn't sure how. Several years ago he'd found a small spot on the riverbank that led to another canyon. If he could only find it again.

Late that afternoon, he almost passed by the little cove covered with brush on the Mexican side of the river. At the last moment he pulled in to shore. Once he docked, it took less than ten minutes to empty the boat and drag all the supplies over the steep hill to the other side. When he was satisfied that all was well and the campsite he'd chosen was right, Dan left Kendra there and went back for one more thing—the raft.

He couldn't leave it in the open for Cowboy to find, nor could he trust himself to hide it well enough not to be seen from the river. He hadn't asked Kendra how good a Herfronite's eyesight was, but neon yellow rubber wasn't hard to see in the dark; once a flashlight was on it, it stood out like a beacon in the night. The raft was their only chance to get farther downriver and survive, but it was also the one arrow that would point to their whereabouts.

It took Dan over fifteen minutes to deflate the raft and carry it back to the camp. Since the foot pump was in his car, which was now in the park another several miles downriver, it would take triple the time to blow it up in the morning.

Meanwhile, he had some questions to ask Kendra. The best way to fight an enemy was to know him. Well, the enemy knew Dan but he didn't have the same advantage. There had to be a way to even the odds.

KENDRA STRETCHED on the top of a sleeping bag and stared at the deep blue afternoon sky. It would be several hours before darkness came and she could see her home.

Internally, she could still feel the shivers that passed through her body. She was afraid, so very afraid. Cowboy had threatened to take both the baby and Dan away from her. In fact, Cowboy wanted her dead. She couldn't believe it. He'd told her that she wasn't a good specimen, that she had broken too many rules and had allowed the human access to the ship; and the slides had been ruined because of her personality flaw. She had to die. What amazed her was that Cowboy expected her to remain where she was until he arrived to do the job. Probably other Herfronites might have obeyed. But not her. Not her and her daughter. And not Dan. Not the man she would protect with her own willful life.

Before night descended, there would be several hours in which she would cook, eat, plan, scheme and love the one person who had turned all her ingrained values topsy-turvy. The one man who made her consider making her home with him.

A week ago, she never would have dreamed of hiding from her own kind. Common sense told her she had to find other Herfronites and beg them to help her establish a rapport with her Elders. Perhaps they could protect her and Dan until she straightened out this misunderstanding.

That brought another question. She had been the first to return to the ship. Where were all the others? What had happened?

No matter what the answers, she knew she had to go home eventually. This short time with Dan was only a reprieve, not the solution.

The others who had come with her might not return to the ship for another night or two. When they appeared, perhaps Cowboy would recant his decision. Perhaps.... But she knew better. The others had nothing to do with changing Cowboy's mind. She wasn't naive enough to believe that fairy tale.

Stones skittered down the hillside and Kendra mentally imagined the person responsible. Dan. Dan with the deflated yellow raft in his arms and fear in his heart. Her heartbeat quickened at seeing him again. He was coming with questions. Well, answers were the least she could give him. He needed answers to make his next decision—whatever decision that was. She hoped it would serve them both well.

Suddenly his mind closed and she couldn't read him anymore. Had he known she was probing? She had tried to be so gentle. She didn't know if Dan realized they had been connected most of this trip. Had he known of her invasion and not wanted her to read his thoughts?

He dropped the yellow bundle next to the sleeping bag and stared down at her.

"We need to talk," he stated grimly.

She knew that already, and was prepared. "You wouldn't let me read you. Why?" she asked bluntly.

"Because I don't know if there's just one crazy Herfronite out there or if others like you may have returned early. If they did, they might *malk* me and tell your fellow Herfronite where we are."

Kendra sat up and pushed her dark hair over her shoulders. He was becoming more logical than she was. "Of course. I didn't think of that."

She hesitated, calming her manner and preparing to do a search herself, to see if anyone out there was responsive to her. After a moment, she smiled. "I don't think we have to worry about that right now. The mountain behind us seems to be a good block to *malking*."

"Good. But the sooner we get away from here, the better off we'll be. The danger is real, Kendra. For both of us."

"I know. I'm so sorry you're involved. I should never have chosen you to pick me up."

"You didn't pick me," he countered. "I chose to pick you up." Her look was disbelieving but he decided to ignore it. "But now I need to get us out of here alive."

"Tell me what I can do."

"I have to know as much about Cowboy as you do. Anything about him could be a clue to eliminating him."

"Eliminate?" Her eyes widened. "As in kill?"

"If necessary."

"I can't let you do that. It would be very wrong."

"We may not have a choice."

"Herfronites do not condone killing." Kendra knew she sounded stubborn, but this was too important an issue to let slide.

"Why don't I believe that? Your Cowboy isn't following either of us for our health, honey. He wants to kill us. You know that as well as I do. We both read that thought correctly or you wouldn't be with me now."

It didn't matter what others did, she could not accept killing. But Cowboy was the exception, and she didn't know why. Maybe they would find out later, when they were in the car and headed toward wherever....

Kendra took a deep breath. Then, with a sigh, she patted the spot next to her. "Sit down and let's talk," she said. "Then we'll see what needs to be done."

Reluctantly, Dan did as he was told, sitting at the bottom end of the sleeping bag. "What is Cowboy's name and how long has he been here?"

"His name is Dirk. He's been here for a long time. Apparently he's watched many shiploads of us come and go. To use an old term in our tradition, he guards the gates."

"Like the devil he is," he said, his thoughts jumping ahead. "His being here a long time means that he could be a rogue."

"What does that mean?"

"Because he's been away from his own kind so long, he might not relate to them. And because he's police for his kind here, he might not relate to new Herfronites, either. If that's the case, he could be working alone, making his own decisions without checking with his superiors to know what he should do."

"No." Kendra shook her head emphatically. "That could never be."

"What would you call it? The man is vowing to kill both of us, and with no reason! You were just showing me around. If he didn't like it, he should have known you could have erased my memory. That would end the problem—at least as he saw it."

"He knew you ruined the slides and I was responsible."

"That still doesn't mean you should die for it."

"And I haven't been following all the rules," she admitted, as if committing a sin were equal to killing.

"Man, you people are tough. None of those offenses are worth death."

Kendra frowned, caught up in Dan's logic. He was right about his thoughts being wiped out. Dan didn't have to die to eliminate the problem. And she was willing to return home, no matter how much she wanted to remain with Dan. Dirk's behavior didn't make sense.

On the other hand, the only explanation that fit was the one that Dan had given: Dirk was a rogue.

An invisible but very real, icy-cold mantle dropped over Kendra's shoulders when she thought of Cowboy pursuing them for no apparent reason. No matter what Dan said, Kendra knew that Dirk would catch up with them. On their own terra, Herfronites were slow, occasionally plodding. However, here on Earth there wasn't as strong a pull of gravity or the heaviness of the air to impede them.

On both planets their minds were clear and concise; the no-nonsense, logical mind of a scientist. All that made Dirk's actions and thoughts a mystery. What was his plan? Why would he want to kill one of his own when Kendra had already *malked* him that she was resigned and reluctantly ready to go home?

Either Dirk wasn't being logical or Kendra was missing a vital piece of the puzzle.

Dan stirred restlessly and turned to her. "If you went back to Herfron, what would you tell your people?"

"It's not if, but when," she reminded him gently, leaning forward in her earnestness to make him understand. "I will go back, Dan, and explain what happened if I can retain my memory. But the answer to your question is that, if I had a chance, I'd like to return and live here."

Turning his head, Dan stared back out at the landscape. Kendra mentally etched his profile into her brain. It was a strong male look, one that made her feel as if he could handle all problems—any problems—except that she knew he couldn't. Dammit.

"Why wouldn't you have a chance? Would they kill you?"

"No. But our normal process is to wipe out our memories on the way home and file them."

"Does anyone have access to these files?"

Kendra watched, fascinated, as a bird alighted on the inside branch of a spindly cactus. "Only the Elders."

"Who makes decisions based on that information?"

"The Elders."

"Well," Dan drawled thoughtfully. "They're not the know-alls you think they are, honey, or they wouldn't allow Dirk full rein. If he goes around trying to kill others, he keeps it a secret. Either that, or they condone everything he does."

"The Elders wouldn't do that."

"Why not?"

"All decisions are based on whether or not something is for the highest good of our race."

"If what you just said is true, your death might be expedient."

"Don't say that," she admonished. But her own fear of his direct dealing with the problem had already done its job. He was right, he was right, he was right, her pulse sang with confirmation. For the first time in her life, she understood firsthand what fear tasted like.

"Dan?" Her gaze locked with his and she tried so hard not to let her fear show.

But Dan understood her needs. His arms opened, enfolding her to his chest, keeping her head comfortingly close to the steady thump of his heartbeat. One hand ran up the inside of her cotton shirt and his lightly callused fingertips soothed the soft skin of her back.

The rhythmic sound reassured her that all would be well. She knew better, but at least his presence delayed the panic she felt bursting through earlier.

Kendra's fears slowly ebbed. Her arms refused to let him go, however; and she opened herself to Dan, allowing him to see her own worries and doubts.

He must have read her, for his arms tightened around her and a frustrated moan echoed from his throat. He buried his mouth in the curve of her neck, caressing her with his warmth.

"It'll be all right," he promised in a low, gravelly voice.

Kendra nodded a silent response, but they both knew better. Even though they'd slipped away from Cowboy this time, he would follow them until he found them. They would have to be constantly vigilant. Until Kendra could get word to the Elders, running from the threat of being killed would be their future pattern.

"We won't have to," Dan stated aloud. "This will end soon."

Kendra gave a shaky laugh. "You're getting good at reading my mind. I'd better watch what I'm thinking."

"Don't block me out, honey." The raspy sound of Dan's voice ran down her spine like chilled wine. "I might find some small fact we could use that you didn't think was important enough to mention."

She smiled and pulled away from the comfort of his chest. With an intense feeling of need and love that made her fingers shake, she framed his face. His skin was warm from the sun, tanned and golden brown. His deep-set blue eyes stared down at her intently with an emotion she couldn't fathom but made her feel warm all over. "Can you tell what I'm thinking right now?" she questioned softly.

His expression changed slowly. "Are you sure?" he asked.

"Very, very sure," she whispered back, almost afraid to move in case she broke the spell that seemed to surround them.

A smile burst over his face and tenderness shone from eyes that delved into hers. "Well, then, little lady, the least I can do is accommodate you."

He leaned her back on the down-filled sleeping bag. Then, in the shade of the Mexican mountains and a tall cactus, Dan kissed Kendra. His touch was tender but possessive, his kiss sweeter than Kendra could ever have imagined. With tantalizing slowness and an equal amount of gentleness, Dan began telling Kendra—wordlessly, with lips and hands—how much he wanted her to stay with him.

Her sighs turned to moans. Still he refused to give her satisfaction or take his own. Kendra was his and this was his way of branding her with his essence. As his tongue circled her peach-tinged areola, her breath caught in her throat.

He realized he was affecting her just as much as she affected him; that she wanted him as much as he wanted her. "Say it, dammit," he muttered hoarsely. "Don't make me say it first."

She knew what he wanted, and she gave it to him. Her hand touched his jaw, lifting his head so that he could stare deeply into her eyes. She wanted him to see the honesty there. "I want you, Dan. I want you so badly I tremble with the need."

Sighing in relief, he enfolded her in his arms and entered her. Her gasp told him she had waited for their coupling as much as he had needed it. Just her touch was an aphrodisiac. The heat of her was more powerful than the setting sun, singeing him with her own special kind of hunger. Trying to maintain control, Dan made aching, intense, wonderfully sweet love to Kendra.

Later, darkness covered them like a black velvet canopy with millions of tiny silver holes in it. He still held Kendra curved close to his side as they stared up at the night sky and she pointed out various stars. She was replacing his memories of his wife with experiences that made real the possibility of a future with her. He realized he was in love with her.

7

IT TOOK ALMOST TWO hours for Dan to inflate the trusty yellow raft. He blew until he got dizzy, stopped, then began again five or ten minutes later. Kendra tried to help, but her lungs didn't have the capacity to blow out a candle at three paces, let alone a raft almost six feet long.

Every few minutes he'd look at Kendra, who spent her free time meditating on a rock at the top of the hill, well hidden from unsuspecting eyes. She was acting like radar, trying to capture a stray thought from Cowboy. Dan was pretty sure Dirk believed they'd continued on their way down river.

Once the raft was packed and ready, he loaded it quickly, then went to get Kendra. Reaching the hilltop, he halted in the shade of a mesquite tree and watched the woman who had changed his life—again. She sat cross-legged, facing the river below. Her body was in a meditation position and her eyes were closed. Her head was tilted like a flower seeking warmth from the morning sun.

Years ago he would have scoffed at someone doing anything New Age, but not now. Now, nothing surprised him. The woman he thought was more beautiful, loving and sweet than any other was an alien. What more could he say?

Oh, it was apparent that she was trying to ignore the fact that she'd be leaving him soon. But he knew. Every moment was borrowed time and he treasured each fleeting second with her. A lump formed in his throat and he coughed to erase it. The sound caught Kendra's attention but the lump remained.

"Are you ready?" Her gaze took him in from head to toe, as if checking to ensure he was all right. She must have been satisfied, because she smiled with loving possessiveness before he could reply.

"You're so beautiful." He hadn't meant to say it aloud. It just slipped out.

"Thank you." She gave a little nod to acknowledge the compliment. "So was your wife."

"No, my wife was pretty, but she was so badly marred by her own problems that she never had the chance to be beautiful where it counted—on the inside."

Kendra's brown eyes turned as golden as the sun as they lit with an inner light. He had given her the supreme compliment—the one meaning *I see your soul and it is beautiful.* Instead of saying a mere thank-you again, she mentally wrapped her emotions around him, letting him know just how deeply she was moved by his words.

Dan didn't move, just allowed himself to submerge in the mesmerizing silence of her feelings as she touched his soul. Without saying anything, he opened his arms, "asking" her to come so that he could hold her physically close.

With a grace and style all her own, Kendra rose and stepped into his embrace. Giving him a hug, she turned and leaned against him, wrapping his arms around her waist and holding them there, as if to feel the solidity they created when united. He placed his open palm on the light swell of her abdomen and knew he was cradling his unborn daughter.

The future was hazy, the past was irrevocable, but the present was right here and right now.

And, right now, Dan was in the place he most wanted to be; with this Kendra wrapped in his arms, in an old land filled with ancient memories, watching a new day being born.

It didn't get any better.

THE TRIP DOWNRIVER was calm. Dan remained on watch, but saw nothing. Kendra was unusually silent, but said she couldn't feel the presence of Cowboy.

Once, they heard voices raised in laughter and knew several rafts loaded with tourists were close behind them. They ignored them. Another time, Dan saw an old Mexican on the hillside boiling cactus to make pulque. Dan waved at the old man and he waved back.

Rapids were more frequent now. They were winding their way into Big Bend National Park toward Santa Elena Canyon, where boulders as large as houses were scattered like building blocks in the narrow confines of a sheer-sided canyon. For most tourists it was the highlight of the rafting experience. For kayakers, it was the ultimate test of skill. It could be dangerous if the ones leading weren't skilled.

Dan thought it was like shooting fish in a barrel—and he was the fish. "We have to get off the river."

"Why? Are we near your truck?"

"No, but Cowboy probably already knows where the truck is, and is waiting for us. When he finds it, he'll think we're still on the river. Our only chance is to outsmart him by getting away from the river, where he expects us to be."

Dan flipped the oar to the other side of the raft and began edging toward the shore. "There's a dirt parking lot over there. We'll see if there's anyone who can give us a ride to Del Rio or Alpine. We can rent a car there."

Once they were on land, Dan took her hand and they walked toward the parking area. A family of six was busily packing up gear into the back and top of a large van. Two youngsters, obviously twins, were squabbling over who was going to get the window seat, while the teenagers seemed too busy breaking down equipment to argue. Ten or twelve more vehicles were parked in haphazard fashion all along the side of the lonely highway. Another van—white with blue pinstriping—sat at the far end.

With a light tug on Kendra's hand, Dan skirted the family. When they finally spotted him, he gave an easy wave but continued on his way to the last car. He tested the doors—all locked. But a bulge on the floor of the driver's side showed that whoever had driven it had tucked the keys under the carpet. The people who owned the vehicle had the door keys only.

Dan turned and frowned, his voice carrying as far as it could without him shouting. "Honey, would you start unloading the raft? I'll help as soon as I get our car open."

She read his mind and he felt her struggling against the lies he was going to tell. Reluctantly, she fed him the lines he requested. "What do you mean?" she asked. "Why can't you open the door?"

"I didn't want to worry you, darlin', but I dropped the key in the river late last night when I was securing the raft. I'll have to break into the car to get our keys."

"Oh, honey," Kendra moaned. "Why were you so careless? I could have put them in my fanny pack, but you insisted on keeping them. Now look at us! Our insurance probably won't pay for the damage, thanks to your carelessness."

"Don't preach at me, honey. I already feel bad enough as it is," Dan retorted, acting frustrated. It wasn't much of a reach. "Just get the gear, okay?"

With reluctant steps, Kendra headed back to the bank. As she passed the family, she gave another look over her shoulder in Dan's direction. He pretended he was busy trying the doors once more just to be sure he'd have to break a window to get inside.

"Lose your keys?" the man called. At Dan's nod, he asked, "Wanna try mine? Sometimes they work."

Dan hadn't thought of that when he began this scenario. If the key worked, it was a bonus. "Thanks. It's worth a try."

Dan tried to hide his impatience as the man sauntered over and dug for his keys in the pocket of his faded orange swim shorts. With a slowness that rivaled bread rising, he found the key chain, picked out the proper key and tried it in the lock. The older man wiggled it, turned it, then grinned widely as the latch popped up. "Happens like that sometimes," he commented with a grunt of satisfaction. "Someone once told me one key will fit every tenth car."

"Well, I'll be damned," Dan said, looking incredulous. Relief flooded him and he tried to convey that feeling to Kendra. He wondered how quickly he could get rid of the man and get the car packed.

The man shrugged but he was visibly proud of his accomplishment. "Wouldn'ta mattered. If this hadn't worked, the wire hanger from my trunk would have done the job," he said. "The missus always does something harebrained with her keys, so I'm prepared just in case. It's what comes of marrying a pretty little air head."

Just then Kendra came up the path with an armful of waterproofed packing and one of the coolers. Dan grinned and waved her over. "This kind man just unlocked our car for us," Dan explained as he reached for the keys under the carpet and pocketed them before helping her with her load.

Kendra waved at the man as he walked back to his car. Her dark eyes glinted with anger over his comments about his wife, but she yelled a friendly "Thanks!"

He waved back. "No sweat," he replied. But his hand went to cradle his temple as if a stabbing pain had jabbed at him. Dan stared sharply at Kendra, but she was still smiling.

"Get in the car," Dan said in a low voice, still with a bright smile on his face. "We're leaving the rest behind."

"That's wasteful," she whispered back.

"That's tough," he contradicted. "Our lives are at stake."

"What about the poor people who own this car? They're going to return and find themselves stranded."

He opened the passenger door and practically shoved her in. "Better for them to be stranded than for us to be dead. Dead, Kendra," he repeated for emphasis. "Not just without a car."

He stuck the key in the ignition and turned it. The engine started right up. Quickly he checked the gauges. They were in good shape. They even had a full tank of gas.

Kendra continued her thoughts aloud. "Yes, but his family will be standing by the spot where their transportation was parked. The children will be hot and tired and the mother will be short on patience."

Dan slipped the car into Reverse, then slammed on the brakes and stared at her in shock. "Can you read the future, too?"

"No, but I can imagine."

He looked at her cautiously. "Can you tell if the man who owns this car is married and has children?"

"No. It's all guessing, Dan. Don't panic. I might be able to read minds on occasion, but that's about it. I don't even do a good imitation of flying."

"Flying?" He wasn't following her thoughts at all. "What kind of flying?"

She grinned. "You know, like the extraterrestrials in the movies."

Dan laughed and put the vehicle into gear.

A little less than an hour later, he glanced down at the odometer. They'd gone only twenty-two miles on the rough dirt-and-gravel road, but were finally approaching the exit area of the park.

"Block your thoughts," Kendra warned suddenly.

Dan did so, praying that Cowboy couldn't feel his fear. With quick precision, he pulled onto the main, paved road that led out of the park and continued to drive at a reasonable speed, his mind on automatic as he felt the faint pinprick prodding of Cowboy's probe. He knew it was Cowboy even before he heard his words: *When I catch you—soon—no one else will know what pile of rocks I buried you under.*

He gave a heavy sigh and looked over at Kendra. She stared straight ahead, her body rigid. The damn man had left Dan alone because he'd found his prey: Kendra. Dan stepped on the gas and bumped over the road at almost a hundred miles per hour. It wasn't his van and he didn't give a damn what happened to it as long as it would run long enough to keep Kendra out of harm's reach.

As the car careered toward the signs that proclaimed the approaching entrance/exit, he glanced at Kendra again. She sat clutching her seat belt at chest level, her wide-eyed gaze on the road in front of them.

He slowed down. "Are you okay?"

"Are we slowing down?"

"Is that what's scaring you?"

Kendra nodded. "It is now. There's more than one way to die, Dan."

He took his foot off the gas pedal and eased to a stop at the park entrance.

"Go right," Kendra prompted. "Toward Del Rio."

"That way is closer to the river," he told her. "If Cowboy continues to ride downriver, he could mentally pick us up as we come closer to the Mexican border again."

"Dirk isn't on the river anymore. He's heading toward San Antonio, too."

"How do you know?"

"He's not the only one reading minds," she said. "He still wants to find and kill us."

Now that they weren't on a death ride, her mind was obviously elsewhere. "You can read *his* thoughts?"

Kendra looked at him, surprise in her expression. "Of course. So did you for a moment, remember?"

"I know, but I thought he was sending me a message."

She stared back out the window. "He can't act on something and mind read at the same time. It's too difficult."

Barely holding his impatience in check, Dan jabbed the steering wheel with his finger. "I mean just now. Did you read him?"

Kendra nodded, her forehead still wrinkled in a frown.

"And?" he prodded.

"He thinks I'm going back to San Antonio because it's the only place I know my way around. Because of the way I feel about you, he also believes you and I met when I first arrived in San Antonio."

"Everything you said is very logical, honey. He's gathering bare facts, then dressing them in assumptions."

"Yes, but he's wrong!"

"Don't be brokenhearted about it." Dan's voice was as dry as the dirt road they'd just traveled. "As soon as he realizes he made a mistake, he'll correct it. Don't forget, this is the guy who's trying to kill us."

He felt Kendra's eyes on him for a long moment, but he forced his attention on the road ahead—and somewhere deep inside himself as he tried to second-guess the man who would soon figure out which route they'd taken. Somehow he needed to outthink the enemy to stay alive.

Four hours later, they reached Del Rio. Dan's shoulder muscles were so tight he thought he'd start shaking and not be able to stop. Kendra sat with-drawn and quiet, hands on her lap, unmoving. For once she wasn't prodding or plotting; just sitting in silence. Dan should have known that it didn't bode well.

When he pulled up to a stoplight, he reached over and covered her hands with one of his own. Her skin was cool and dry. "What do you want to eat, honey?"

"Nothing."

He withdrew his hand and turned into a fast-food restaurant driveway, parking in a spot across from the entrance. "Well, I'm eating here. If you want some-thing, let me know now."

Kendra's hands wrapped around his arm, clutch-ing at him as if he were about to disappear right in front of her. When she looked up at him, he was stunned by what he saw: stark, unadulterated fear shone from her eyes like a neon beacon. "Please, don't leave me. Please."

He rubbed her hands, spreading his warmth to her. "Shh, it's all right," he reassured, knowing he was as nervous as she was but pretending otherwise. "Do you know something I don't know, Kendra?"

She shook her head, her coal-dark hair glinting with reflected sunshine. "I don't know anything. I don't understand what's going on, and that frightens me more."

He wrapped his arms around her and rocked her back and forth the way his mother had done when he'd had nightmares as a child. His heart hurt from the pain Kendra was suffering, but he didn't know what to do about it.

"Poor baby," he crooned, inhaling the very special scent of her and loving it. "Your world is so logical and structured that it's a miracle you've survived so well in this crazy one."

She sniffed. "I don't understand any of it. Especially this . . . this feeling."

"Now that you're cut off from your own people, you're just plain scared," Dan explained in a soothing tone. His hands stroked up and down her spine, trying to warm her body the way he'd warmed her hands. "What you're feeling is fear, honey. Pure fear. It just takes time to get adjusted to it."

She nuzzled closer to him. "I'll never get used to it." Her voice sounded muffled against his chest.

He heard the threat of tears in her voice and had to hold on to his own temper. "You will if you stay here long enough," he told her. "You're just a little unprepared for this human life, Kendra." He pulled away from her. "Come on, let's get something to eat."

Less than fifteen minutes later, they were speeding down the highway toward Uvalde. Dan munched on his second cheeseburger, occasionally sipping on a giant iced tea. Kendra sat next to him, daintily eating a salad that looked like it was made for King Kong. What amazed him was that she'd eaten one at the restaurant and had two more on the floor of the car.

"Keep that up and you'll have to go on a diet," he commented.

"I think not," she said in an equally dry tone with a hint of humor.

So far, no one had arrested them for stealing a vehicle. Cowboy hadn't found them. And Kendra was doing better. Overall, Dan thought they were doing pretty well.

He'd never realized just how gentle a soul Kendra was until today. He'd been too busy comparing her to the other Kendra. But the more time he spent with her, the more he knew he'd shortchanged her. She always searched for a peaceful solution. Dan knew that wasn't the case in his life.

She'd also rolled with every punch landed in their direction. And while his gut instinct was to protect this Kendra, experience with her by his side had shown him that she could protect him, too. To Dan, that was amazing. No one had ever protected him before. It was a strange, unsettling feeling, one he wasn't sure he liked. Her intelligence level was astounding; she absorbed everything immediately and understood it in a working, day-to-day way. But street smarts weren't part of her life or training. Also, he was beginning to realize that it wasn't as imperative for her to live through this mess as it was for her to do everything right and fairly, according to Herfronite standards.

If they were getting out of this alive, it was going to be a struggle. Dan had a lot on his hands.

He wasn't sure when the real owners of their stolen vehicle would report the theft. Since this was the end of a weekend, chances were that the van would be reported stolen sometime today. Since he didn't want to steal another one anytime soon, his best bet was to get as far away as he could, and as fast as possible.

When they reached the small town of Uvalde, he decided to change tactics. For lack of a better plan, he pulled off the main highway to San Antonio and headed cross-country toward Pearsall.

"Where are we going?"

"Read my mind," he answered, taking care to circle around a slow-moving truck.

Kendra hesitated a moment, then sat back. "I knew we were headed for Houston, but this doesn't make any sense. This way will cost us a few hours extra—hours we don't have to lose if you use the main freeway."

"If I use the main freeway, I stand a chance of being spotted by the police. Besides, that's exactly where Dirk will think we are. Let's surprise him." *And ourselves*, he thought to himself, for he had no idea where he was going other than back to his apartment. But once there, then what?

"Do you think he knows who I am and where I'm from?" Dan finally asked.

"I'd say there's a pretty good chance."

"But you're not sure."

"I'm not sure."

Dan stretched in the seat, trying to find a softer place. He was exhausted and his body was stiff from the long drive. But he couldn't give in to any pleasures of relief right now. He had to constantly remind himself that he was running for his life. *Their lives.*

He glanced over at Kendra. She was finishing her last salad and dabbed at her mouth daintily with a napkin. Then she placed the container neatly in the bag and sat back. Her legs were crossed in yoga fashion, her back rigid and eyes staring straight ahead. He had the feeling that she was searching for Cowboy.

"He's not close, Dan, but he is following us," she pronounced ten minutes later. "His resolve hasn't changed. He still wants us dead."

"We figured that. At least he's not hot on our trail, yet," he stated grimly. "Relax and enjoy the ride while you can, honey. I'll need you rested for later."

She nodded, then pretended an indifference he knew she didn't feel as she took in the rolling landscape.

Until then, Dan hadn't realized just how tense he'd been while he waited for her to tell him what he'd already known. It didn't change anything, so he might as well take a piece of his own advice. With a heavy sigh, he leaned back and forced the tension from his shoulders.

Five minutes later, a look in Kendra's direction confirmed she was asleep. It was just as well. He might need her help driving, later on. One of them had to be alert and he had a feeling that in an hour or two he'd be unable to keep his eyes open.

Darkness came and the small, two-lane highway took them through little Texas towns that hadn't changed in thirty or forty years. After Pleasanton, they hit Stockdale, then aimed up toward Gonzales. But before Dan could reach the thriving little metropolis, his eyes were closing every two or three minutes. He drove through a little town called Nixon, then pulled onto a dirt road just north of it. After going a mile, he realized they were on a horseshoe street leading to a few old farmhouses. When it ended back on the highway, Dan knew he'd found a temporarily safe place to rest—he'd noticed one small, white framed house that had seemed deserted. He made a U-turn and swung back onto the gravel road. Turning out the car lights, he let the moon direct them to the shale driveway of the darkened house and pulled in. He rolled down both windows and took a deep breath of the hay-fresh night air.

Kendra was still asleep. Tomorrow morning he could fight dragons if he had to, but not tonight.

With a heavy sigh, Dan leaned back and closed his eyes. He reached over and took one of Kendra's hands in his, then fell instantly asleep. But the demons that had pursued him all day followed him right into his dreams. . . .

8

THE SOFT CRY of a kitten woke Dan out of his sound sleep. Early dawn registered as he opened his eyes and looked around. It took a moment to orient himself and remember where he was. Then he saw Kendra sleeping in the seat beside him, and he knew instantly.

The whimpering sound was coming from her. Even though she was still asleep, tears rolled down her cheeks. But what hurt Dan the most was her intensely sad expression. A lump formed in his throat and he had to swallow hard. Still, it wouldn't dislodge.

Filled with an overwhelming gentleness he didn't know he was capable of anymore, he curled her into his arms and let her rest her head against his chest. She didn't waken as he moved her, but the soft crying sounds stopped and she snuggled into the warmth of him.

What had he gotten into? The answer was as ready in his mind as the question had been. He knew. For years he'd been in love with another Kendra—his fantasy of Kendra. Mentally, he gave her wonderful, Superwoman-type attributes, building her into a woman he thought he'd needed but one she could never become. But he'd never been satisfied with their relationship. Even though they'd married, he'd felt a gnawing hunger in his soul that he couldn't explain. When their marriage broke up, Dan realized that his wife had felt that sense of dissatisfaction, too.

Both had built dreams of what happiness meant, and neither had attained it living with each other. Instead of that knowledge drawing them closer together to seek what they were missing, he for his part had become bitter, then had swallowed that bitterness because he couldn't allow himself to get angry with a mate who had "mental" problems; it wasn't the right thing for a "good guy" to do. But that bitterness hadn't evaporated as it was supposed to. Instead, it had festered in the dark corners of his mind.

Until now.

Now, thanks to *this* Kendra, he understood so many of those same emotions he'd glossed over before—not only his wife's complicated ones, but his own, deep-seated feelings that he'd even hidden from himself. His dad used to say that the less a man delved into "woman stuff"—meaning thoughts and feelings—the happier a man was. Until last week, Dan had thought his father might have had a point. Now he realized that if he'd taken the time to explore those same thoughts and feelings earlier, he might not have been so unhappy all these past years.

The counterthought was that if he hadn't met *this* Kendra, he might not have known just how much he had been missing in a relationship. The kicker was that he would soon lose this Kendra, too. She wasn't happy away from her kind. She wanted to find a way around Cowboy and return home.

No matter what, he was going to love and miss her for the rest of his life.

A small, regret-filled sigh escaped her full lips and she turned, her arms circling his waist as she gave his chest a kiss. Still asleep, her actions showed just how close they'd become. She trusted him. Did she love him, too? Or was she this way with every man? He hoped it was for him, but he knew better than to expect it. Being with this Kendra had taught him to expect the unexpected.

For the next half hour, Dan held her in his arms and pretended they were just an ordinary couple on their way home from a camping trip, who had stopped to snuggle and enjoy the Texas sunrise.

A few minutes later, Dan's own eyes closed and he fell into a light sleep. But his arms never lessened their grip on the woman he loved.

WHEN KENDRA FINALLY woke up, she found herself wrapped around Dan as if he were the only life support in the middle of an ocean. That wasn't too far from being right; without Dan she might be dead now.

Kendra wasn't sure, but she had a feeling that Cowboy was just what Dan had labeled him—a rogue. Judging from what she'd felt and *malked*, he'd been down here for over eight years, ruling according to his own justice. She remembered her training in statistics that had shown almost twenty-five percent of the Herfronites sent down to Earth did not return to her planet. The most common cause for this was death. Originally, she had assumed it was accidental. In fact, that thought had been indirectly promoted by her teachers. Did any of this have to do with Cowboy? Now, she had reason to think so.

There had to be a way to find another Herfronite and make some kind of connection that would bypass Cowboy so she could get home. And she had to do all this while keeping Dan safe. If anything happened to him, she had an idea she would break every rule. Without him being safe, she would lose all will to live.

She needed to find a way to keep both of them alive, so Dan would be safe and she could return to her own home. Right now, she didn't have a clue as to how she would accomplish either goal.

WHEN KENDRA WOKE UP again, her head was resting on Dan's lap, her body curled into a human fetal position. Dew and sweet hay blended together with the scent of soap that Dan had used to wash his clothing. She focused her gaze on the dash, silently registering that they had to stop for gas sometime soon. They had less than a quarter of a tank left.

"Did you have a good sleep, honey?" Dan asked, his voice as cheerful as a morning sunrise.

She couldn't say why, but his tone irritated her. That was as surprising as everything else. She wasn't supposed to be irritated by the little things; it wasn't the Herfronite way. But, there wasn't time to ponder this puzzling attitude. Their lives were at stake.

Sitting up, Kendra ran her fingers through her hair, trying to comb it into some semblance of order. It didn't help much. "I had a wonderful sleep," she drawled. "How about you, darlin'?"

Dan looked a little surprised at her comeback, but he must have decided to roll with it. "Wonderful. Now, if we can make it home in one piece, I'll consider myself the luckiest guy in the world."

"Your home," she corrected.

He looked even more surprised. "My home what?"

"If we can make it to *your home*. *My* home is a little more distant."

He didn't say anything but she felt his withdrawal. He didn't want her home to be different or separate. He wanted her to be just like him—or like his other Kendra. She couldn't be. That was someone else. Even if she wanted to be from Earth, she wasn't, she *malked* gently.

"Don't humor me or act as if I'm some idiot needing to be calmed." His voice was a growl.

"I wouldn't dream of it," she murmured sweetly.

"And don't tell me things you think I want to hear." His voice was still filled with anger.

"Of course not," she said softly.

"I just want the truth," he stated harshly.

"Really?"

"Of course," he snapped.

She smiled and turned toward him so he could see how relaxed she was. "Then stop being the world's biggest jackass. You're arguing with the one person who is in this with you. I have just as much at stake in this as you have. Our lives."

Dan's anger slowly ebbed away. It was replaced with a sheepishness. "I'm really that bad?"

"Yes."

"Are you as damned angry as I am right now?"

"No." She sighed, resigned that she would have to go further to resolve whatever he was feeling. Ap-

parently Dan had to understand everything and took
nothing for granted—not even her opinion.

"Why?"

"Because Dirk is doing what he thinks is his job.
Having to kill must be a very heavy burden on him.
Herfronites don't kill."

Dan looked at her as if he'd never understand her
compassion for a killer. "He doesn't seem to be having a hard time to me, honey. I think he's used to this
now."

She shook her head to emphasize her answer. "No.
Herfronites don't even think of killing. It's not a part
of us. We are not a violent race."

"Either Dirk is a killer or he's insane. It really
doesn't matter, since he's on our tail and wants to kill
us."

Kendra had to admit that he was probably right.
She looked thoughtful. "Maybe."

"No maybes about it. We're not the first for him."

"Perhaps not."

Dan was silent for a moment, chewing over that
point. "Kendra, what are your weapons on Herfron?" he finally asked.

"We don't have weapons."

Dan's patience was nearing an end. "Then what do
you think Cowboy will use to try to kill us?"

"Most likely a gun, since that seems to be the weapon of choice here on Earth." Kendra hesitated slightly. "However, there have been so few killings on Herfron that I forgot one or two things. The truth is that we do have a couple of weapons on Herfron, although they're seldom used."

Dan was all business. "Could he have one of these weapons?"

"I don't know. Anything is possible." She took a deep breath. "Yes. He has to have one. You see, although it can be used as a weapon, it's really a medical tool that helps heal us from whatever is wrong."

Taking a calming breath, Dan began again. "Try to take a stand, here, honey, and let me know your thoughts on this weapon's possibilities."

Kendra brushed an invisible speck from the seat between them. "You don't have to get angry with me. Herfronites are logical and telepathic. That doesn't mean they have all the answers."

"I'm not angry," he declared, his blue eyes blazing with just-denied emotion. "I'm simply asking for an educated guess about the man who wants to kill us. After all, he's from your planet, not mine. You know something and you're unwilling to tell me what it is."

Kendra sighed and looked down at her broken nail. Surprisingly, it had begun to grow. Odd to think how many human attributes she was acquiring. . . .

"Stick with me on this, Kendra," Dan prompted. "What weapons?"

He was reading her almost as well as she could read him. She was delaying the inevitable. "The one I'm thinking about is something that looks similar to a television remote control and works very much like a laser. If it's in proper running condition and put on the right controls, it can either stun someone for a minute or so, or kill them. It can even turn a body into dust immediately. It's like a beam of light that is so strong it can eat through any nonreflective material in a matter of milliseconds."

Dan whistled. "Every man's dream. The ultimate remote control."

"But I'm not sure that Cowboy would have one of those."

"Why not?"

"Because they're so intricate and dangerous there are only a handful of Herfronites who carry them. I've only worked them once or twice in training. We didn't even receive one when we came here."

"He's probably got one, then. After all, his prime purpose is to keep you in line."

Instead of answering, she grew thoughtful. How unusual. She always felt so calm, knowing the absolute social and lawful parameters handed her by the Elders. Now, in the less-than-two weeks she'd been on earth, she had also learned to be her own person, and that was becoming even more confusing. Perhaps it was because she'd never completely absorbed the original Kendra's memory. To compensate, her own personality filled those emotional holes, creating an entirely different person from the one she was or the one she pretended to be. The new person was the Kendra she was now.

And with this knowledge came an awareness that Herfron might not be the perfect world she'd portrayed it to be. Rethinking those same walls and rules, she now realized there might have been two sets of rules—one for her kind, and one for the Elders. So many things she'd thought to be true had been proved different this past week and a half. Could her own perception of her people be wrong, too?

She'd certainly been taught wrong about the people of Earth. They were not always a demanding, destructive race without the ability to think logically. Their sun was warm on the skin and they reveled in it. Their colors were vivid and they wore them as decoration as well as lived surrounded by them. Their building skills were superb and it showed in buildings, homes and bridges as well as in parks, playgrounds and recreation facilities. Adaptability seemed to be a byword, and human ingenuity showed it in the thousands of different everyday products available.

They might be babies in their ignorance of the universe, but that wasn't where their drive for knowledge was focused—unlike Herfronites. And in recognizing these differences, she also felt the guilt of not being loyal to the very people who gave her the opportunity to know the differences.

But she had to admit that knowledge aloud. It was the correct Herfron thing to do. "I might have been just a little naive about Earth and humans at the beginning of this trip, but I'm catching on quickly."

"Really?" he asked dryly. "I hadn't noticed."

"Don't get smart, Dan, or I'll erase your memory," she threatened, but her voice held a teasing quality.

"Can you erase bits and pieces?"

"No. Alas, it's all or nothing."

"Then I'll behave." He shot her a grin, but there was an emotional distance in his gaze. "At least until we get Cowboy off my back and you have a chance to return to your own planet, since that's your plan."

Even though that was her ultimate goal, it hurt to hear him say those words. As much as she needed to get back to her people and share what she'd learned, she hated leaving him.

Instead of voicing those feelings, Kendra nodded. But her gaze took in his profile and indelibly sketched it in her memory. Instead of making him look scruffy, his two-day-old beard reminded her of the pictures of dangerous pirates she'd seen. He could even pose for one of the romance novels on the stands in supermarkets and drugstores. His nose was straight, his eyes held delightful crinkles that women would have lamented were crow's-feet. He was a very good-looking man; one any woman would be proud to be with—most of all, her.

That thought surprised her. Was she thinking she was woman first? They didn't have names for male and female on her planet. Everyone was simply Herfronite. Everyone was equal. How odd.

Dan's arm stretched across the top of the seat and his fingers nestled in the nape of her neck. "Thank you," he said.

"How did you *malk* what I was thinking?" she asked, startled at how complicated her feelings were becoming—especially when she knew she was being read by him. She thought she'd blocked. Now she had an idea how he felt when she did it to him.

"You were staring at me with a small smile on your heavenly mouth. I gathered you were thinking about me and it was either pleasant or kind. I chose to think it was kind."

Kendra's shoulders relaxed. "Oh." Her skills at blocking were still intact.

He withdrew his hand and she felt bereft of his warmth. But she refused to reach out and take it back. That would set her up for rejection.

Dan's words interrupted her reverie. "Humans have ways of reading people too, Kendra, and it's not always bad."

"I never said it was." Her speech was stiff. Her body even more so. She clamored for his masculine touch, and the more she wanted to be with him, the more she feared her own emotions and retreated from him.

"You didn't have to. No matter what we are, honey, we aren't inferior, just different."

"Really?" She raised a brow and looked him over. "I never noticed."

He grinned, knowing her dander was up and loving it. "Yes, you did, and you pointed it out all the time."

Kendra stared out the window, not saying a word. He could just *guess* where her thoughts were leading, but she'd be *damned* if she'd tell him.

Dan pulled into a small gas station just outside a charming Victorian town the sign proclaimed was Gonzales. He stepped from the car and Kendra watched carefully as he handed the owner a credit card and started pumping gas. This was risky, since their car might have been reported stolen. Kendra caught the thought that the older gentleman had a citizens-band radio in the office. When business was slow he picked up truckers' signals from the highway.

She was about to delve into the rest of the station owner's thoughts when a highway patrol car pulled up behind them. Holding her breath, she searched for Dan. His body was stiff with tension, his motions jerky. Mentally she reached out to him, soothing his thoughts with the promise that she would find out what he needed to know. Once he was calmed, Kendra turned her talents on the policeman.

The young man was angry about something his wife had done that morning. It wasn't really important except that she'd always done it and it had always irritated him. He'd taken the police car home last night and hadn't seen the official list of things he was supposed to do at the office until just a few minutes ago. Everyone seemed to be dumping on him.

But when he looked at the license plate, Kendra knew that something was wrong—although the man never put his thoughts into words other than a very succinct *Damn!* He walked over to Dan before Kendra had a chance to prepare him, and began talking. Dan looked surprised, then angry. But whatever was going on, she felt he was carrying it off.

By the time he got into the car Kendra could barely suppress her own curiosity. Both Dan and the policeman had done a very effective job of blocking her, and what little she had understood didn't make sense.

"What was that all about?" she asked.

"We've got a Handicapped license plate." Dan spat the words through clenched teeth.

She wasn't sure what that was or what it had to do with their problem. "But what did the policeman want?"

"He wanted to make sure we didn't use a special parking place unless there was a handicapped person in the car. We weren't supposed to take advantage of the emblem."

She felt as if she was waiting for a punch line, but Dan was quiet. "That's it?"

Dan nodded, still staring into his rearview mirror.

"Then let's get out of here." She leaned back, wanting as much space between Dan and the policeman as she could get. Meanwhile, if she was going to protect him, she had to make some changes.

"My sentiments, exactly."

Kendra didn't relax until they were ten miles outside of town on old Highway 90 heading toward southwest Houston.

"Dan, leave me at the outskirts of Houston," Kendra requested in a firm voice.

Dan's voice was equally firm. "No way. You're with me to the end, honey."

"It isn't logical," she argued. This is your world, you need to function in it. If I'm not around you, Dirk will be torn on how to search. That will give you time to hide. Whatever, we need to be separate to improve our chances."

"Herfronite logic doesn't always work on Earth, darlin'. If Cowboy found my Jeep, which I think he did, then he knows exactly where I live. My insurance papers are in the glove compartment with my address printed all over them. He'll know where we're heading and what possible routes to take. And he won't hesitate to use deadly and immediate force."

"I didn't know," she said softly, surprised that insurance papers would be kept in a car while all other records were kept in courthouses on microfiche—or so she'd been taught. Her lessons hadn't gone far enough, obviously. There was so much to learn and so little time to learn it. "If that's the case, wouldn't it be more logical to go somewhere else to hide?"

"Houston is my territory, honey. Cowboy is out of his element there. If I went to another city, we'd both be out of our element and neither of us would have an advantage." He looked at her, his sharp eyes taking in her white face as she realized how dangerous their situation was. "Mark my words, this is a fight to the death—for the both of us. He won't stop until we're dead and we won't be able to live without fear until he's gone. Either way, someone will die."

"No."

Dan didn't respond. He knew she was denying the violence. But there was no other way.

Kendra found herself praying with every turn in the road. She prayed that they would all get out alive, but most of all, that Dan would live and love again. He deserved it. With all the bad things that had happened in his life, he deserved a love that knew no end.

Kendra opened her mouth to argue, then tensed. She'd felt a probe again. "Get ready," she said quickly, then shifted her mind to the bland, gray countryside of her own planet. She could feel Dan's body tense as he readied for the first onslaught.

With a deliberateness bred into her from birth, she soothed her own emotions. It was the best she could do under the circumstances. She was so filled with love for Dan and fear for both their lives. The probe, weak as it was, came again.

Dan's foot was heavy on the gas pedal as they sped through another small town. She was going to tell him to slow down but was afraid to put it into words. The probe would come again, she was sure, and she needed all her concentration to filter it through without allowing it to pick up on her or Dan.

She took a deep breath and concentrated hard. She was ready. Shock filled her senses, stilling her quickly beating heart.

The probe was not Cowboy.

"Slow down," Kendra ordered quietly.

It took Dan a minute to register what she'd said and lightly step on the brake.

"Stop," she told him. "Pull to the side of the road."

Dan's brows lifted almost to his hairline. He looked at her, then back at the road. "Are you crazy? I don't have a suicide wish, and I won't let you have one, either."

"Please, do as I say," she said, trying desperately to keep the weak connection.

Cursing under his breath, Dan pulled to the shoulder of the road and sat tensely, watching Kendra. He hoped he could catch a thought in midstream and save her from the pain. Instead, she ignored him and focused on *malking*.

Minutes ticked by as slowly as hours for Dan and he fidgeted in his seat while he waited impatiently. Kendra tuned out completely, focusing only on the person she was relating to.

And she was amazed.

The *malker* was a man planting a field nearby. He'd been on Earth for over nine years, having come here as part of a farming experiment she'd never heard of.

He was a Kau, a second-generation Herfronite, and wished he was as far along genetically as she was. According to him, his short legs and heaviness, typical in a Herfronite, were a detriment on Earth. Because of his internal differences, doctors considered him to be an oddity. He was only glad he wasn't color-blind, like the Elders.

There were others, he said. They had found a way to live with humans without the Guardians finding them. They didn't call attention to themselves or keep in touch. Each had formed his own underground connections and they met occasionally. But that was all. No one wanted more than to be human and to be left alone. When the Guardians found them—which happened occasionally—they disappeared.

Dan picked up a stray thought or two and was just as shocked as Kendra. Was the whole world going crazy?

She asked the farmer several questions about the Keepers or Guardians, finally letting him know that one was chasing them. In his years on Earth, no one had ever come after him.

An instant later, he pulled his thoughts away and closed down any connection between them.

"What happened?" Dan asked, demanding an answer.

But Kendra didn't have one. It was unbelievable to her that some of her kind had stayed here on Earth. Why had the Elders allowed that? Where were the Guardians? Was the farmer right and were there more Mais and Kaus still living in this world? If so, where were they? And what did they *do?*

On Herfron there were committees or co-op work programs that benefited all. Many worked for more than one and took joy in the prospect of working so hard. But it was different here; everyone was an individual, doing his or her own "thing," as they referred to it. How could Herfronites live like humans?

"Stop looking at the differences, honey," Dan said, and she knew he was reading her mind. "Look at the similarities."

Kendra saw a sign proclaiming Houston as being thirty miles away, but her thoughts were still on their discussion. Dan's ideas were food, adding to her own newly forming opinions. "I don't understand, Dan. Everyone here is an individual, a freethinker, yet they act much like Herfronites when they band together for a cause."

He shrugged. "I told you we were similar."

"Maybe. I'm not sure," she murmured absently. "Right now, I wonder how many of my kind are here. And why is Cowboy only after us instead of someone like the farmer?"

"Apparently we teed him off," Dan stated dryly, but she could tell he'd wondered the same thing. "He has a tail on us, and he knows you're pregnant."

"But why us?"

"Who knows? We could have ticked him off or his superiors could be angry with him and we're the most accessible. Or maybe it's because we ruined an experiment."

"My heavens, I never would have believed this could happen. We could be dead because he was able to trace our whereabouts."

"But I'll see him dead before he harms you."

It was stated with such icy-cold, no-nonsense conviction, a chill ran down Kendra's spine. "That's not right," she protested softly. "No one should kill."

Dan was about to answer, when the first probe entered his head. As individual as facial features or fingerprints, the probe was identifiable.

Dan stepped on the gas and raced toward the distant skyline that revealed downtown Houston. He was fighting for their lives.

Cowboy was back.

9

DAN DROVE AT BREAKNECK speed toward the Houston city limits. The narrow, two-lane road they had been traveling blended with another and soon they were speeding up the Southwest Freeway toward a tall clump of buildings on the far horizon.

Cowboy's probe, now gone, had been weak. But it had been a chilling reminder that he was still hot on their trail. The time for confrontation was approaching fast.

Kendra rested her hand on Dan's thigh as if physical contact with him would keep him safe. She was at a complete loss; it wasn't just the fear for her life, either. It was her feelings for Dan. Was she in love with him?

Kendra knew the answer, but refused to acknowledge it aloud.

She loved him more than her own life.

She looked at Dan, hoping he would give her some kind of reassurance, some small grain of hope that all would be well.

There was none.

White-knuckled fingers clenched the steering wheel. Dan's face, usually relaxed, was as taut and clenched as Kendra felt. Narrowed eyes gazed into the future. His mouth was uncompromising, his jaw rigid.

She tried to gently probe his mind but it was closed.

"Stop it," he barked.

Kendra withdrew. "Don't cut yourself off from me, Dan. Let me in."

"Not now, honey. I can't always be sure it's you. Cowboy might change his tactics and be gentle enough to slide through my own barriers. Then we'd be dead ducks soon afterward."

Dan was an optimist if he seriously thought he could stop the Guardian. "You don't really think we have a chance against someone like him?"

He nodded. "All we have to do is figure out why he's after us, and then we can nail him on it."

Kendra's laugh was dry. "Of course. Why didn't I think of that?"

Dan's sigh echoed through the van. "I didn't say it would be easy. I said it was what we needed to know."

A new emotion flowed through Kendra's thoughts. Panic. Didn't Dan realize just how final fighting the Herfronite Guardian could be? Instead of running and evading him like the farmer did, Dan wanted to stand and fight. It was all wrong, she was sure. "He's too powerful. If he wasn't, the farmer would have continued talking to me."

"The farmer was scared, honey. He was protecting his family and his way of life. Under the circumstances I'd do the same thing."

"You?" She shook her head in denial. "I don't think so. You'd probably take your trusty pitchfork and head toward trouble, ready to defend your home and hearth to the death. Isn't that what you're planning to do, anyway?"

Dan's grin was strained, but at least she'd gotten him to respond. "Not quite, honey. I want to live, not look like an artist's rendition of a painting in a museum."

Kendra turned toward him, touching his arm in her effort to impress her own thoughts upon him. "Then let's run. He may be unable to follow us outside the state. You can go anywhere. You can start again."

"Let's get this straight. You're saying 'we,' but what you're really talking about is running with me until you find a way back to your own planet. Right?"

Kendra winced. The words sounded worse aloud than in thought. She tried to pretend those same words were all right, but it hurt to think of leaving Dan almost as much as it hurt to think of never returning home. Most of all, for her own protection, she had to remain aloof from the emotions that threatened to take hold of her spirit and bind her to the only human who could hold her here.

"Right?" Dan pressed again.

"Right," she said on a resigned sigh. She hoped he would leave the subject alone, but she knew better.

His own matching sigh echoed through the van and Kendra waited for some kind of outburst or show of anger.

There was silence.

She probed, ever so gently.

There was no thought she could pick up.

"Dan? Are you all right?"

"Fine." The word was snapped out, curt and short. "We're being chased by an assassin and I'm fine."

"Talk to me, Dan," she pleaded in a low, soft voice. "Let me know what you're thinking."

Looking worn-out, Dan ran a hand through his hair. "This whole damn thing isn't fair. We have to fight to stay alive, and if we win, my reward is that you'll leave me. If we lose, I get to die with you."

Tears formed in her throat, clogging her breathing. She swallowed, then touched him again, trying to convey silently just how hard this was for her, too. But he had retired from her words and emotions again.

It was time for plain speaking. "You and I might not like the outcome, but I can't see it any other way, Dan. We're from two different planets, for God's sake! This isn't a problem that can be solved by seeing a marriage counselor! It's not something we can say we'll work out as we go along."

"Why not?"

"Because," she began, but the words didn't come. "Because." She halted again. Thoughts weren't coming, either. "It would never work."

"What a profound statement," Dan countered with disgust. "You're the mother of my child and I love you so damn much I hurt from it. Why would it never work?"

She stared out the front window, dejected because she couldn't argue his points, and torn because she knew he was right but she didn't want to confirm it. "Because you're looking for something I can't give you."

"What? Commitment? Trust? Loyalty?" he asked. "Love?"

"Something like that," she finally managed, knowing she could give him all that and more.

He grew silent in retaliation.

But angry or sad or disgusted, Dan took her breath away. Until she'd come here and absorbed half of Kendra's thoughts and wants and desires, it had never dawned on her to want for herself all those intangible things he was talking about. Now, something had gone wrong and she'd filled in the parts that Dan's nating—mesmerizing her into slowing down. She looked around the well-lighted food court that was three stories tall. It was as noisy as a circus, as light-bright as a new hospital, more colorful than a long trail of magician's scarves.

Dan returned, grabbed her hand and pulled her through the lines forming to get into restaurants. "Come on!"

They ran down the length of the city mall, darting among customers and clients in a mad dash toward . . . Kendra didn't know where.

Suddenly a zinging sound echoed in the building, whizzing closely past Kendra's ear. A display window next to them shattered and crashed to the floor in a thousand pieces. People screamed, a child cried.

Heart racing, her hand clutching Dan's, Kendra kept running. With a jerk, he pulled her onto a set of stairs that moved downward. "What are these?" she yelled as he continued to pull her toward the bottom.

"Escalator!" he shouted back, pushing an Armani-suited man and a heavyset woman to the right. "Emergency! Make way!"

They ran down the rest of the steps, taking the last several two at a time. Green marble floor ran like a carpet, guiding the way through almost six miles of the tunnel system that connected most of the important office buildings downtown. Tan carpet-covered walls muffled their running steps as they passed others going to and from work. Several women, dressed in office suits and sneakers, momentarily blocked their path as they turned a corner and ran into them headlong.

Dan looked over his shoulder, but the crowd barred his view of Cowboy. Then, a shattering of glass caught his attention. The bagel man standing by his food cart cursed loudly; his silver canvas top had smoke billowing from it. The silver must have deflected Cowboy's laser because there was also a black spot on the ceiling that lazily billowed smoke.

Heart racing so hard he could hardly hear his own voice, Dan pulled Kendra after him. "Run!"

The rich green-tiled floor turned to a dull brown. Ceiling lights changed from modern bullet insets to large rectangular fluorescents. Dan led her into a drugstore, almost mowing down a screaming toddler attempting to yank away from his mother.

"There's no exit," Kendra told him breathlessly.

Panting, he stopped, staring at a blank wall where the outside door should have been. "How did you know?"

"Someone told me." She looked around even as Dan dragged her up one aisle and down the other, searching for the one who had *malked* the information. If her emotions hadn't been so overloaded already, she might have stopped again and tried to reason out what was happening. Instead, she flowed with it and began leading Dan out. *Where are you?*

I'm shopping with my children, the malker answered. *Keep running. He's just entered the store and is looking down the right aisle by Cosmetics.*

Kendra gave a quick glance at the signs posted from the ceiling and found the section Cowboy was in. Then she pulled Dan after her. They slipped through the exit turnstile and continued to run down the hallway.

Another thought was *malked* to her. *I see him coming out of the store. Run and get out of here! Through the bank!*

Kendra was stunned by the thought. It wasn't the same woman who was in the drugstore, but another female Herfronite somewhere in the tunnel. *Where's the bank?* she asked, but the answer wasn't quite clear.

Farther down.

What are you doing *here?* she asked frantically as she ran down the hall.

Same thing you are—living, came the answer. *There are more.*

Kendra didn't have time to reply. Dan had taken the lead again and turned down a corridor toward an empty copy shop. They could hear their own footsteps as the noisy crowd was left behind. They turned down another hallway and one more. Then they stopped. It dead ended in a small square area with several doors and an elevator.

Their heavy breathing bounced against the walls and floor, sounding like an echo chamber.

Dan jabbed at the elevator button several times but there was no whirring sound that proclaimed a moving car. Kendra looked around. There were two rest rooms, a door without anything written on it and a set of double doors. A loud dull hum generated from the room beyond.

Letting go of her hand, Dan ran from one door to another, rattling the knobs. Nothing opened.

A scream echoed eerily from somewhere down the main corridor. Dan turned again to the double doors. With all his strength he shook and pulled on them until they popped open, exposing an air-conditioning and heating utility room. It was a long room, filled with round pipes big enough for men to climb through. Painted in various crayon colors, the insulated pipes lined the floor, crawled up the walls to the ceiling, then jutted off in every direction.

"Damn," Dan muttered, knowing he had no place to turn. This would be the showdown site. He pushed Kendra down on the floor between two pipes. "Stay there and keep your head down! And don't let him see you, no matter what!" he ordered. Then he closed the

able to avoid a direct hit, but the chopping motion still had an impact.

The Herfronite yelped, took another step into the room, stumbled, pulled his arm away and regained his balance. A smile framed his mouth as he aimed the laser toward Dan. "Where is she?"

"Gone."

Dirk sent a knife-sharp pain straight to Dan's head. "Where is she?" he repeated.

Dan gritted his teeth and took a deep breath, barely able to contain the pounding in his brain. "Nowhere you can get a hold of her, you son of a—"

Kendra heard Dan's cry of pain even before she raised her head to look. Bright red blood was quickly spreading into a large dark stain that dampened his jeans-clad thigh.

Anger flooded every pore in her body and she could taste her desire for revenge. Acting on instinct, Kendra stood in defiance, clenching nothing in her fist to fight the man but a banged-up beer can.

Dirk had shot a defenseless man—the man she loved. She faced Cowboy, hatred on her face.

"Kendra! No!" Dan yelled. Everything he felt for her was in his eyes as he frantically tried to protect her with his own body. He took a step forward to come between them, but stumbled over the pipes.

Overwhelming fury surged through Kendra. Cowboy had hurt Dan. *He'd hurt Dan!* She wanted to strike back, to hurt Dirk. She wanted to kill him.

Cowboy turned toward her, his mouth the wicked semblance of a smile. "Ready?" he asked, in a conversational tone. "Pleasant dreams."

Then he aimed his laser at Kendra.

"No way!" she cried, holding the can out in front of her just as he flipped the switch on the laser.

The shiny aluminum can deflected the laser back to the doorway, just as it had done on the bagel man's umbrella.

Quickly, Cowboy shot again.

Kendra instinctively corrected her aim.

Smoke sizzled out of Cowboy's chest. His hands laced over the wound. His look was as incredulous as hers was. He stared at Kendra, then, in slow motion he turned his head toward Dan. His mouth opened, but whatever he had to say was never spoken.

Kendra watched in stunned disbelief as Cowboy sank slowly to his knees, all the while staring up at her in wonder. He shook his head. *I don't believe it*, he *malked*. Then, slowly, his eyes closed and he fell over.

Kendra's knees gave way and she dropped to the cold concrete. She stared at the man on the floor between her and Dan. At the same time a crackling sound vibrated through the room until the air-conditioning system swallowed it up.

"Kendra." Dan's voice was quiet, but it caught her attention. "Dear God, Kendra."

Still stunned, she gazed over at him, at first unable to understand the magnitude of what she had just done and unwilling to accept either the blame or the credit. She ran a hand through her hair, pushing it back from her face. "Sweet heaven, what have I done?"

Dan's voice was so low she could hardly hear him. "You did what you had to do, honey. If you wanted us to live, you had to kill him. I tried, but I couldn't."

"But to kill . . ." Her thought drifted off. Since she had met this human, she'd gone through so many changes she couldn't count them anymore. As shocked as she was by what she'd done, that wasn't what appalled her the most.

She had been lied to by her Elders. There were lots of Herfronites on this planet. She had been here only two weeks and she'd met four of them. Two of them had come forward just now and helped save her life. They lived and worked here! It wasn't an accident that she'd found them; they had sought her out to help her run away from Cowboy. That told her there were probably more. Lots more. Perhaps that was what had happened to some of the ones who had traveled with her. They had decided to pull away and didn't want her to know so she couldn't turn them in to someone like the Guardian, Cowboy.

"Kendra, talk to me," Dan said softly. "Damn, honey. Don't leave me in limbo about what you're thinking."

She gave him all her attention. She was alive and well. Her baby was still safe inside her. And Dan was alive. That was most important.

Her hands shook as she reached out to help him stand. Breath hissed between his teeth at the pain in his thigh, but they both knew he would make it. He would mend. So would she.

She grinned outright. Her thoughts were churning again—telling her she had the means to make him whole—the same "weapon" that had killed Cowboy. "Wait a minute," she said, reaching for the control. She studied it carefully, trying to remember the vague instructions given her several years ago. She pushed a series of buttons, and suddenly the code she wanted popped into the small viewing screen. "Hold on," she told him, carefully placing the scanner on the floor and easing Dan's pant leg away from his wound.

"Damn," he said between his teeth. "Careful, honey. That's the only right leg I have."

"Now don't move," she ordered, picking up the scanner again and aiming it at his leg.

His hand clamped on her shoulder. "Do you know what you're doing?"

"More than you do," she retorted, suddenly businesslike. "You're bleeding pretty badly and it has to heal fast if we're going to get out of here before some security or maintenance man finds us with a dead body at our feet."

He still looked doubtful. "You're sure you're not going to finish the job your friend started?"

Her laugh came just before the jolt to his leg, and he braced himself for the pain. As much as it electrified his system, it didn't hurt. Instead, it tingled.

After a few seconds, she took her finger off the button and leaned back on her heels. "Feel okay?"

Surprised at the reaction, he nodded. "Fine."

"Move your leg."

"You sure are bossy when you hold the controls," he muttered, but he did as he was told. His brows rose. "It feels fine."

She grinned, then stood. "Good. Can you walk?"

He tried it. It was stiff, but didn't hurt.

With a smile still on her lips, she slipped the scanner in her sweatshirt pocket and turned once more to look down at the body draped over the pipe. It was a horrible reminder of how close they had come to death....

Feeling exactly the same way, Dan groaned, shutting his eyes to the horror as he wrapped her in his arms and felt the soft strength of her. "You're still smiling. We must be alive."

Kendra laughed in relief. "We're alive."

Dan continued to hold her tightly. Finally, the big chase was over. "Looks like we won, *kemosabe*."

"*I* won, you chauvinist!" She gave him a light punch in the stomach. "Now you owe me a white hat."

His lopsided grin made her heart do flip-flops. How human could she get?

"In that case, my darling alien, I'll buy you a dozen," he promised. Together, they stared down at the definitely dead Herfronite. In death the man had lost his long lean shape and become puffy and bloated. Slowly his body was flaking, turning to dust. In an hour's time there would be nothing but gray flakes to show where he'd been.

"Dan, I—"

"Funny," Dan mused, not taking his eyes off the man who had hunted them down so relentlessly. "When he was alive, he could eat Clint Eastwood for breakfast. But now—now he looks like a giant Pillsbury Doughboy with hair."

"He's a Kau," she reminded him solemnly. "A Herfronite. So am I."

His hand possessively tightened around hers. "I know. I remember. I love *you*, my darling. Him, I'm not too fond of. Thank God we're the ones that are alive," he muttered, visually checking to make sure she was all right. With fingers that shook, he stroked her face, neck and shoulders. She was safe. He was safe. He'd never doubt miracles again. Maybe God would even grant him one or two more....

THEY WALKED THROUGH the tunnel and through The Park shopping-center door. Once there, Kendra aimed the scanner at a woman who was walking toward them, her sad face painted with a plastic smile. Within a few seconds, the woman continued on with her shoulders straightened and the smile no longer painted, but real.

"Why did you do that?" Dan whispered.

"Since I don't have the correct combination code to keep it working, it will lose its power in a day or so. That woman had cancer. The darn thing might as well help someone while it works. She's cured."

"Her doctor will tell her it's a miracle cure."

"And to her, it will be," Kendra confessed. "Why not?"

Dan hailed a cab, purposely leaving his own Jeep and the stolen van at the curb. The cops would bring his back and he would pretend he knew nothing about the thefts. Kendra read his mind and for once didn't chastise him for doing the wrong thing.

When they reached his apartment, Kendra walked in and looked around. "This reminds me of my own habitat. Plain and functional."

"Thanks," Dan stated dryly, trying not to let on just how nervous he was having her here. "It needs decorating, but I'm not good at that kind of stuff."

She turned and put her arms around his neck, curling her body into his. "Well, then, we ought to do what you do best."

His body stirred immediately as the adrenaline that had poured through his system so readily over the past three days continued to pump.

"Lady, you know just what to say to make me feel better."

He made love to her as if it were the last time. Indeed, he didn't know what was going on in her mind and was almost afraid to ask, for fear she'd tell him she was leaving. Just the thought acted like a hand clamping off his breath, bringing pain to his heart and tears to his eyes.

The rest of his life without Kendra? *This* Kendra. Oh, he knew the difference now. Looks were the only thing that tied this woman to his dead wife, and even those had slowly changed. Their personalities were so opposite, they were like two different women. The woman in his arms was the woman he loved as a grown man—a grown man who would deeply love only one woman in his lifetime. If there was life after this Kendra left him, he didn't want to imagine what it would be.

His loving was gentle and tender, then changed to passion that said without words just how much he loved her. And her own movements suited, then fit his. Whatever the tempo, she matched him. Neither read the other's mind; neither had to. With every thrust, he branded her as part of him for all time. She answered each of his time-honored commands with a demand of her own. They were evenly matched and equally in love. He'd swear by it.

Later, as Kendra nestled in the safe harbor of his arms, his heart cried silent tears. He wanted to hold her forever. But reality intruded and questions banged at his mind, demanding he get the answers. Not knowing what was going on in her mind was worse than knowing the impending direction of her thoughts.

He finally asked the question uppermost in both their minds: "What now, Kendra? Are you going home or staying with me?" he asked softly, finally placing the problem between them. "What happens to us?"

Her legs stirred, but she kept her head resting on his chest. She hesitated for only a second before answering, "I can't leave you now, Dan."

His breath came out in a whoosh.

Kendra continued. "For some reason you've turned into my whole life, and I can't—won't—give you up ever again. Besides, our daughter deserves to know her birth father."

His sigh was warm against her cheek. "Thank God," he murmured. His fingers stroked her skin as if she were pure gold. "I love you so damn much, honey, that if anything had happened to you, I might as well be dead, too."

His mouth covered hers in a kiss that melted through to the very core of her. Her arms encircled his neck and she clung to him for support. The feelings only Dan could ignite in her were too wondrous to give up. When she finally pulled away from the kiss, she looked at him with eyes languorous with desire. "Now that I know what this strange emotion is called, I can honestly say that I love you, too," she said. "It's been there all along, you know. Ever since I first met you."

He ran his thumb over her bottom lip. Strange, it was much fuller than the original Kendra's. "Darlin', those words just won you a marriage license. Or it will, as soon as we forge a birth certificate for you."

"Why?"

"So we can prove you were born here on Earth."

Kendra's eyes widened in understanding. "That's not a problem. I was given one when I was brought here. It's all ready to fill in the necessary blanks—depending on the information of the person I was to become."

"Just one more problem solved in the long list of dilemmas of living with an alien," he teased, and his hands still cupped her face as if he was unwilling to part from her.

But Kendra wanted him to understand the terms fully. "There are others of us here. I spoke to two of them in the tunnel system. If I stay on Earth, I will maintain contact with others of my kind, Dan. Other Herfronites. Perhaps someday we can all come to terms with our Elders."

He grinned. "I should have known. Your organizational skills at work. Before long, you'll be organizing bridge nights with them, talking about the joys and problems of raising human kids."

Her laughter was free for the first time since they'd left her spaceship. "What else do you expect from a bossy, independent housewife?"

"Nothing less," he answered softly. "Absolutely nothing less."

Kendra reached for his hand and kissed his palm. It was time to begin their life. "Are you sure you're up to this, Dan?"

"I'm sure." His voice held conviction. The dark light in his eyes emphasized his tone.

A sigh of relief escaped her lips. "Well, then." An impish twinkle lit her big brown eyes. "If I'm going to learn to be a housewife, I should begin by doing all those things your women do during the day, like redecorating your apartment. I saw this magazine and it had the sweetest nursery...."

She laughed at his groan. She knew he was glad to be alive. Glad to be with her.

They both were glad. Strangely enough, she'd gotten out of the habit of using the "we" that linked her to her fellow Herfronites. Now she was "we" with Dan; "we" with just one other instead of a whole race.

And she loved it—probably because she loved him and knew she was loved in return.

"We'll make a home with our love," she whispered, placing a light kiss on his jaw. *"Our home."*

They both knew that whatever they did, whatever mistakes they made or ordeals they had to overcome, they would do it together. Forever.

His smile was her reward.

Temptation

brings you...

THE HART GIRLS

Bestselling Temptation author Elise Title is back with a funny, sexy, three-part mini-series. **The Hart Girls** follows the ups and downs of three feisty, independent sisters who work at a TV station in Pittsville, New York.

In **Dangerous at Heart (Temptation August '95)**, a dumbfounded Rachel Hart can't believe she's a suspect in her ex-fiancé's death. She only dumped Nelson—she didn't bump him off! Sexy, hard-edged cop Delaney Parker must uncover the truth—or bring Rachel in.

Look out for Julie Hart's story in **Heartstruck (Temptation September '95)**. Kate Hart's tale, **Heart to Heart**, completes this wonderful trilogy in October '95.

Available from W.H. Smith, John Menzies, Volume One, Forbuoys, Martins, Woolworths, Tesco, Asda, Safeway and other paperback stockists.

MILLS & BOON

are proud to present...

A set of warm, involving romances in which you can meet some fascinating members of our heroes' and heroines' families. Published each month in the Romance series.

Look out for "Make-Believe Family" by Elizabeth Duke in August 1995.

Family Ties: Romances that take the family to heart.

This month's
irresistible novels from

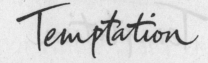

FORMS OF LOVE by Rita Clay Estrada

Lost Loves mini-series

Dan Lovejoy had lost his wife in a tragic accident when he met her double. Only this woman who looked like Kendra wasn't Kendra. Dan couldn't help himself; he started to fall in love with her. But this woman had some very *unusual* secrets of her own.

CHRISTMAS IN JULY by Madeline Harper

Ali Paxton Bell had more than Christmas on her mind when Sam Cantrell came to town. Sexy and charming, Sam definitely had a twinkle in his eye. And one hot, steamy night he paid Ali a visit she wouldn't forget in a hurry…

STRANGE BEDPERSONS by Jennifer Crusie

Nick Jamieson wasn't the right guy for Tess Newhart. He was caviar and champagne and she was take-out Chinese. He wore tailored suits and she wore faded jeans. He wanted to get ahead and she wanted…him. Great sex wasn't enough to build a relationship on—was it?

MADELEINE'S COWBOY by Kristine Rolofson

Madeleine Harmon was finally going to visit the West—take sunrise breakfast rides, have adventures and watch the desert stars. Only she got picked up by the wrong man at the station and found herself taking care of Stuart Anderson's ranch and his lonely young daughter.

Spoil yourself next month
with these four novels from

Temptation

DANGEROUS AT HEART by Elise Title

First in *The Hart Girls* trilogy

Life wasn't easy for Rachel Hart. Single and pregnant, at least she had had the good sense not to marry the no-good father of her child! Things couldn't get worse, she assured herself. Then her ex-fiancé turned up dead. And Rachel was the prime suspect...

A KISS IN THE DARK by Tiffany White

Notorious playboy Ethan Moss wasn't exactly what Brittany Astor had been fantasizing about for years. Temporarily blinded, Ethan was hiding himself away from the world. For timid, plain Britt this was her chance to have a hot and torrid fling with him. But what about when fantasy time was over?

GHOST WHISPERS by Renee Roszel

Alice Woods wasn't frightened of Theora, Percival Castle's resident ghost. Everything would be fine—if only she could ignore Nick, the mysterious stranger who was in her thoughts far more than her ex-fiancé. But ignoring Nick wasn't going to be easy, especially after Theora arranged for Alice to share Nick's bed...

HAPPY BIRTHDAY, BABY by Leandra Logan

Karen Bradford was shocked. Her baby, who she believed had died at birth, had been put up for adoption. Now she learned her daughter's name was Wendy. She lived with her father— sinfully sexy Ross Chandler. And suddenly Karen didn't know who she wanted more...

GET 4 BOOKS AND A MYSTERY GIFT

Return this coupon and we'll send you 4 Temptations and a mystery gift absolutely FREE! We'll even pay the postage and packing for you.

We're making you this offer to introduce you to the benefits of Reader Service: FREE home delivery of brand-new Temptations, at least a month before they are available in the shops, FREE gifts and a monthly Newsletter packed with information.

Accepting these FREE books and gift places you under no obligation to buy, you may cancel at any time, even after receiving just your free shipment. Simply complete the coupon below and send it to:

HARLEQUIN MILLS & BOON, FREEPOST, PO BOX 70, CROYDON, CR9 9EL.

No stamp needed

Yes, please send me 4 free Temptations and a mystery gift. I understand that unless you hear from me, I will receive 4 superb new titles every month for just £1.99* each postage and packing free. I am under no obligation to purchase any books and I may cancel or suspend my subscription at any time, but the free books and gifts will be mine to keep in any case. (I am over 18 years of age)

2EP5T

Ms/Mrs/Miss/Mr _____

Address _____

_____

_____ Postcode _____